PRAISE FOR THE NOVELS OF
Kay Hooper

SLEEPING WITH FEAR

"Hooper's Special Crime Unit novels all have their own unique blend of mystery, suspense and the paranormal laced with a touch of romance. The author is a gifted teller of action-packed stories."
—*Romantic Times Book Reviews*

"Suspense just doesn't get better than Kay Hooper's novels . . . it's a one-sitting read that will hold you in its grip from beginning to end."
—*Romance Reviews Today*

"An entertaining book for any reader."
—*Winston-Salem Journal*

"Hooper keeps the suspense dialed up. . . . Readers will be mesmerized by a plot that moves quickly to a chilling conclusion." —*Publishers Weekly*

CHILL OF FEAR

"Hooper's latest may offer her fans a few shivers on a hot beach." —*Publishers Weekly*

"Kay Hooper has conjured a fine thriller with appealing young ghosts and a suitably evil presence to provide a welcome chill on a hot summer's day."
—*Orlando Sentinel*

"The author draws the reader into the story line and, once there, they can't leave because they want to see what happens next in this thrill-a-minute, chilling, fantastic reading experience." —*Midwest Book Review*

"This definitely puts Ms. Hooper in a league with Tami Hoag and Iris Johansen and Sandra Brown. Gold 5-star rating." —*Heartland Critiques*

HUNTING RACHEL

"A stirring and evocative thriller."
—*Palo Alto Daily News*

"The pace flies, the suspense never lets up. It's great reading." —*Baton Rouge Advocate*

"An intriguing book with plenty of strange twists that will please the reader." —*Rocky Mountain News*

"It passed the 'stay up late to finish it in one night' test."
—*Denver Post*

FINDING LAURA

"You always know you are in for an outstanding read when you pick up a Kay Hooper novel, but in *Finding Laura* she has created something really special! Simply superb!" —*Romantic Times* (Gold Medal)

"Hooper keeps the intrigue pleasurably complicated, with gothic touches of suspense and a satisfying resolution." —*Publishers Weekly*

"A first-class reading experience." —*Affaire de Coeur*

"Ms. Hooper throws in one surprise after another. . . . Spellbinding." —*Rendezvous*

AFTER CAROLINE

"Harrowing good fun. Readers will shiver and shudder." —*Publishers Weekly*

"Kay Hooper comes through with thrills, chills, and plenty of romance, this time with an energetic murder mystery with a clever twist. The suspense is sustained admirably right up to the end." —*Kirkus Reviews*

"Peopled with interesting characters and intricately plotted, the novel is both a compelling mystery and a satisfying romance." —*Milwaukee Journal Sentinel*

"Kay Hooper has crafted another solid story to keep readers enthralled until the last page is turned."

—*Booklist*

"Joanna Flynn is appealing, plucky and true to her mission as she probes the mystery that was Caroline."

—*Variety*

AMANDA

"*Amanda* seethes and sizzles. A fast-paced, atmospheric tale that vibrates with tension, passion, and mystery. Readers will devour it." —Jayne Ann Krentz

"Kay Hooper's dialogue rings true; her characters are more three-dimensional than those usually found in this genre. You may think you've guessed the outcome, unraveled all the lies. Then again, you could be as mistaken as I was." —*Atlanta Journal-Constitution*

"Will delight fans of Phyllis Whitney and Victoria Holt." —*Alfred Hitchcock Mystery Magazine*

"Kay Hooper knows how to serve up a latter-day gothic that will hold readers in its brooding grip."

—*Publishers Weekly*

"I lapped it right up. There aren't enough good books in this genre, so this stands out!"

—*Booknews* from The Poisoned Pen

"Kay Hooper has given you a darn good ride, and there are far too few of those these days."

—*Dayton Daily News*

BANTAM BOOKS BY KAY HOOPER

The Bishop Trilogies
Stealing Shadows
Hiding in the Shadows
Out of the Shadows

Touching Evil
Whisper of Evil
Sense of Evil

Hunting Fear
Chill of Fear
Sleeping with Fear

Blood Dreams

The Quinn Novels
Once a Thief
Always a Thief

Romantic Suspense
Amanda
After Caroline
Finding Laura
Hunting Rachel

Classic Fantasy and Romance
On Wings of Magic
The Wizard of Seattle
My Guardian Angel *(anthology)*
Yours to Keep *(anthology)*
Golden Threads
Something Different/Pepper's Way
C.J.'s Fate
The Haunting of Josie

KAY HOOPER

~

Illegal Possession

BANTAM BOOKS

ILLEGAL POSSESSION
A Bantam Book

PUBLISHING HISTORY
Bantam Loveswept mass market edition published March 1985
Bantam mass market edition / April 2008

Published by Bantam Dell
A Division of Random House, Inc.
New York, New York

This is a work of fiction. Names, characters, places, and incidents
either are the product of the author's imagination or are used
fictitiously. Any resemblance to actual persons, living or dead,
events, or locales is entirely coincidental.

Bantam Books and the rooster colophon are registered trademarks
of Random House, Inc.

ISBN 978-0-553-59053-1

Printed in the United States of America
Published simultaneously in Canada

www.bantamdell.com

OPM 10 9 8 7 6 5 4 3 2 1

Illegal
Possession

ONE

SHE CHECKED THE line for the third time and then swung out over the guttering, lowering herself cautiously until her feet were firmly placed on the lintel protruding slightly above the top window. She had no fear of being seen from within; this was the attic window, a round conceit fashioned in bogus stained glass and certainly opaque from paint if not from plain old dirt. Her soft kid boots gripped the stone securely, and she looked down over her shoulder to pinpoint her target one last time. Yes—there it was: a raised window sash on the second floor.

Her gaze continued downward until she noted the grass directly beneath her, noted indifferently and with but a glancing thought how that grass would welcome a body falling five stories into its grasp. It would have been easier, she thought, to climb up to the second floor rather than climb down to it, but inconveniently placed shrubbery lighting cast a distinctly unwelcome spotlight on the entire first floor. Only a suicidally bold thief would have taken the chance.

Troy was bold—but she was also shrewd and cautious. And luckily she could belay herself down faster and more quietly than nine out of ten men could have climbed up. Decision made.

Balancing easily on the narrow ledge, Troy reached up to roll down her ski mask to cover her face. That done, her gloved fingers moved automatically over her compact tool belt, ticking off each tool in its proper place. Then she gripped the line, expertly bent her knees, and pushed away from the building, swinging out and down with the speed and control of an experienced mountain climber. The first fall took her down to the third floor, her booted feet touching the brick wall with the lightness of a feather and the silence of a cat.

Knees bent, she allowed her joints to absorb force and sound for a split second, and then pushed off again.

Her second jump took her exactly to target: the open window sash was at waist-level and to her right. Again, flexed knees took the force of her landing, absorbing sound. Troy paused for a moment, head turned and eyes fixed on the sentry who'd just rounded the corner of the building. She watched in silence, not a sound betraying her to the man or to the alert Doberman that was pacing on a short leash at his side. Both passed her position, some feet below her, and moved on, the man swearing quietly to his canine companion about the absurdity of patroling on a night as cold as a witch's broomstick and as black as the Earl of Hell's waistcoat.

Troy turned her head to watch them move out of sight around the opposite corner of the building. She saw mist rise in front of her eyes and realized absently that she'd held her breath, but her lungs hadn't complained; Troy could hold her breath for a long time. She locked the line in position and used the niches in the bricks to pull herself sideways until she could peer between the crack in the drapes.

She had highly developed night vision so her eyes saw as much of the interior of the room as was possible through the narrow crack. A chair, a desk, what looked like a game table, and—ah! Books on shelves. The plans had been worth what she'd paid for them then; this was the library. The safe should be to the left of the desk and probably—unoriginally—behind a painting.

She braced her feet even more carefully and slid a hand inside the open window. Sensitive fingers gloved in form-fitting kid searched slowly and delicately for any indication of wire or trip device, and found none. Still cautious, Troy unhooked a small electronic device from her belt and pushed a button, her eyes fixed unwaveringly on a small green light as she moved the device all around the window frame.

A moment later Troy returned the device to her belt, her brows lifting silently and invisibly behind the ski mask. No alarm system. Then it was true that the man relied on his patrols and dogs for protection. Odd, she thought. But maybe not so odd. This man was somewhat new to the acquire-art-at-any-cost breed; his collection probably wasn't extensive enough yet to demand state-of-the-art protection. Or perhaps he just hadn't realized that he could be a target.

Behind the ski mask a smile appeared, and Troy let it have its way. *By this time tomorrow night*, she thought with real amusement, *he might be calling me to rig up a security system for him.* That thought almost brought a giggle, but hanging two floors up on a line suspended from the roof wasn't quite the place to indulge in humor. Troy swallowed the giggle and got on with the job at hand.

Slender, startlingly powerful hands slid beneath the sash, gripped, raised. With a silence born of long practice she lifted one leg over the sill until she was sitting astride it. She unhooked herself from the line, making sure that it was within easy reach outside the window, then swung the other leg over and straightened up inside the room.

She stood for a moment, allowing her eyes to adjust to the very slight difference in the texture of the darkness, then moved swiftly. Avoiding furnishings as though it were her own living room, she crossed to the door and stood for a moment with her ear against it. Silence. Turning away, she produced a pencil flashlight and pointed it toward the floor, going back to lower the window to its former position and completely close the drapes: Troy took no chances with a sentry's wandering gaze. Only her rope remained outside, and it blended in perfectly with the wall.

In seconds she was standing before the painting she'd expected to find. One sweep of the light showed her that it was a rather commonplace print, and she grinned again behind the mask. What thief would bother with this painting? Only one who suspected something behind it! A brief inspection told her that the man didn't stint on inside protection: the framed print was wired. After a moment's thought she rolled her mask back up and placed the narrow flashlight between her teeth, reaching for tools and getting to work.

In a space of time that would have embarrassed a certain security company, Troy had the alarm disconnected and the hinged frame swung open to disclose the safe behind it. And with a speed that would have won the admiration of half the safe-crackers in the world, she opened the safe. Still holding the flashlight in her teeth, she reached in and swiftly found what she was looking for. The painting was rolled up in a cardboard tube. She grimaced. Granted, that cardboard tube made things easy for her, but to treat an Old Master this way...

And then the lamp in the corner spilled golden light over the room.

Troy had only a few seconds in which to think and plan, but it was enough: she was nothing if not quick on her feet. Holding the painting again rolled up and ready to slide into its tube, she turned her head toward the door and studied the intruder with an insolence not a whit marred by the flashlight still gripped between her teeth.

He was dressed in pajama bottoms and a robe, and seemed disgustingly wide-awake and aware for two A.M. Well over six feet tall, he had thick black hair brushing his collar in back, shoulders that a football player would have envied, and a face that half the women Troy knew would have murdered spouses to have lying on the pillow next to theirs. It was a lean, intelligent face with keen eyes that were presently staring at her with a sort of fascinated wonder, high cheekbones and firm jaw, and a mouth that was curved with innate humor and more than a spark of sensuality.

Troy had never seen him before, and was

reasonably sure that he wasn't a resident. In her five days of studying the layout of the house and the comings and goings of its occupants, he hadn't crossed the threshold. Just her luck, she groused silently, that he'd turn up for the night and then go looking for something to read!

Making the best of things, Troy grabbed the ball and ran with it. Taking the flashlight from her mouth, she hissed, "Shut the door."

Automatically he did so, then seemed to collect himself. "What the hell—" he began.

"Shhhh!" she hissed again. "You want to wake up the whole house?"

Unconsciously whispering, he said, "I think I'd better."

"Don't be ridiculous." Troy calmly closed the safe and hid it behind the print, still holding the painting and cardboard tube in one hand.

"Now, look—" he began in a fierce whisper, but she cut him off again.

"You're not a friend of the owner of this house, are you?"

Advancing a little farther into the room and placing himself absently or by design (Troy thought the latter) between her and the window, he glared at her and answered, still in a whisper. "No. He wants me to join him in a business venture, but—" This time he broke off himself, looking somewhat bewildered. "Why the hell am I talking to you instead of calling the police?" he demanded in a wrathful mutter.

Troy ignored that. "I wouldn't take him on as a business partner if I were you," she advised, her voice not a whisper but still soft enough to be mistaken for one.

The stranger stepped closer, looking her up and down with an expression that covered a wide range of emotions—surprise, bemusement, appreciation, anger. Clearly he was seeing the definitely feminine attributes advertised by her form-fitting black sweater and pants, and the delicate features that would have dazzled a movie mogul, and was wondering what a girl like her was doing robbing a safe in the dead of night.

Before he could give voice to his emotions, Troy unrolled the painting and displayed it in front of her. "He wouldn't be very trustworthy, you know," she told the stranger conversationally. "The master of the house, I mean."

Shifting his eyes from her face, the stranger sent

a cursory glance down at the painting. Then his gaze grew intent. He stepped closer. "Isn't that—"

"Yes, it is. Stolen from a private collector in Paris two weeks ago."

The stranger stared at her as she began rolling the painting back up. Then he seemed to feel that some defense of his host was called for. "John couldn't have known it was stolen when he bought it," he said a little uncertainly.

Troy laughed softly. "Bought it? Well, I suppose you could say that. He paid a man to steal it for him."

The stranger pounced. "How do you know?"

Coolly she answered, "Because the collector paid me to steal it back. And since he's a very well-known and trustworthy man, I'll take his word over your John's any day."

"He isn't my John," the stranger corrected irritably. He stared at her for a long moment. "Why don't we just call the police and turn the matter over to them?" he suggested mildly.

Troy strolled over to the desk and leaned a hip against one corner. Swinging her leg idly, she smiled at the suspicious stranger. "Why don't we? Go ahead—do it. I might have to spend the night in jail, but once this painting is identified and my employer contacted, John'll be the one explaining things to the police. If he sticks around, that is."

Her challenge met with a cautious response; the stranger didn't go near the phone. "I can't just let you leave the house with that painting," he said finally. "How do I know you're telling the truth?"

"You don't."

"Well, convince me, dammit!" he snapped softly.

Troy couldn't help but smile wider. She cocked her head to one side like an inquisitive bird. "You wouldn't have gone into business with him, would you? I don't think you trust him."

"That's beside the point," he said.

"Hardly."

He glared at her.

Troy returned his glare with a thoughtful look, then nodded slightly as she came to a silent decision. "Okay then; since you won't trust me, I'll trust you."

"What's that supposed to mean?" he inquired warily.

She held out the cardboard tube. "You take it. Put it under your pillow or in your suitcase or something. If John calls the police in the morning, you'll know he's legit and that I lied. If that happens, wipe your fingerprints off this tube and drop it in the umbrella stand, where it'll be found quickly."

The stranger made no move to accept the painting. "And if he doesn't call the police—assuming, of course, that he discovers the painting gone?"

"Oh, he'll discover it gone. I'll bet he drools over it every morning and again before he goes off to bed. He's probably built—or is building a secret room down in the wine cellar for this first acquisition and all those he hopes will follow."

"And so?"

"And so, when you find John at breakfast tomorrow morning gnashing his teeth and hear him giving his security people hell—and not bellowing about his loss over the phone to the police—you'll know he was responsible for having the painting stolen initially or that he was well aware of the fact he'd made an illicit purchase. Then, if you decide to trust me to return the painting to its rightful owner, we can meet somewhere."

The stranger appeared to be nearly as quick at

making up his mind as Troy was; he reached out to accept the painting. "An honest man," he said ruefully, "wouldn't hesitate to call the police."

"Scruples are hell, aren't they?" she noted sympathetically.

"Do you have them?" he asked ironically.

Cheerfully Troy said, "I used to. But it occurred to me that I was missing a lot in life, so I threw 'em away."

Baffled fascination grew in his dark eyes. "Who *are* you?"

Troy made a slight gesture that a Shakespearean actor would have envied in its controlled insouciance. "Just a thief passing in the night."

"Quit it," he ordered irritably.

Amused, Troy realized that he was fast on his way not only to condoning, but even defending her chosen occupation. Swallowing a giggle, she fought hard to infuse her voice with an air of mystery. "Where shall we meet? In a dark, dingy bar with greasy cutthroats glaring in shifty-eyed malevolence?" She warmed to her theme while the stranger gazed at her in baffled silence. "There'll be a man with a face like a bulldog tending the bar, and the clientele will look as if they belong on the Ten Most Wanted list, and nobody will meet our eyes when we look at him. Mr. Big will be in the back room with his hit men, and he'll have one of them peer through a two-way mirror to make sure we're not wearing white hats. And then—"

"Enough already!" The stranger groaned softly.

Solemnly Troy said, "Not your type of habitat, I gather. Oh, well. Then we'll just pick up our lamps like what's his name and go in search of an honest man. What say we meet on the steps of the Lincoln Memorial?"

"What's your name?" he demanded, ignoring all else.

She lifted an eyebrow at him. "Don't you mean my alias?"

"Dammit!"

In her relatively eventful life Troy had learned many useful lessons, not the least useful of which was that it wasn't safe to wave a red cape at a bull on the point of charging. Somewhere after that lesson came the one about taunting strange men. So she quit while she was still in one piece.

"I'm Troy. What about you?"

"Dallas," he murmured. "Dallas Cameron."

There was a moment of silence. Reflectively Troy said, "Better known as 'Ace' Cameron—because you always have an ace up your sleeve in a business deal."

He looked startled. "You've heard of me?"

"Even cat burglars read the newspapers," she explained apologetically.

Dallas Cameron ran fingers through his hair in a gesture probably originated shortly after man first met woman. "You are the damnedest—Troy what?" he demanded suddenly.

"Just Troy."

"Now, look—"

"As interesting as this little meeting's been"— she cut him off calmly—"I really should be on my way. One of the security men checks this room every two hours, and his last check was an hour and a half ago. I'd suggest you go back to your room and forget that you were in here tonight; if the security man finds you after I've gone, your host is apt to be rather suspicious in the morning."

"How are you getting out?" Dallas asked, staring at her. "For that matter, how'd you get *in*?"

"Turn off the light and I'll show you." Before

he could reach the switch beside the door, she added, "Wait a second," and removed the small flashlight from her belt again. "Better take this so you won't bump into the furniture. Point it at the floor if you don't mind."

Accepting the flashlight, he muttered, "And if I do mind?"

Ignoring the disgruntled question, Troy waited serenely for him to follow her requests. Commands? When darkness had once more claimed the room, she waited until the darting beam of light—pointing toward the floor, she observed with amusement—reached her. Then she moved silently toward the window. She pulled the drapes apart and slid one leg over the sill, leaning out and reaching for her line.

Dallas barely had time to note these activities before she had disappeared through the window. Startled, he only just remembered to keep the flashlight hidden inside before poking his head out the window. "What—"

"Shhh." It was only a sibilant whisper, as were the words that followed. "Don't move. Don't make a sound."

He could just make out her face in the darkness, and his eyes slid sideways and down, following the direction of her gaze. Into his line of sight came a guard and a vicious-looking Doberman.

In his place at the head of a boardroom table Dallas "Ace" Cameron was a man widely known for his nerves of steel. Nothing, both friends and enemies had said at various times, had ever shaken his iron composure. But now, as his eyes followed the progress of the watchman below, Dallas felt his heart stop.

Here he was, leaning out of his host's library window in the wee hours of the morning, holding a stolen (from whomever) painting in one hand, a thief's flashlight in the other, and highly conscious of the woman clinging to the brick wall to his right with the ease of a damn fly. And when the watchman chose to dawdle leisurely directly below them, Dallas felt his heart begin to beat again. It sounded like a jungle drum to him.

He also had to sneeze. Badly.

For an agonizing moment the watchman remained directly under them, his voice reaching them in the cold night air as he complained absently to his companion about lousy working conditions. It seemed to be an old refrain to the

Doberman, because he paid little attention to his handler. Instead, he gave Dallas a very bad moment by sniffing around the bushes close to the house.

But then the guard had called the dog to heel, and they wandered on around the corner of the building. Dallas let himself breathe again, conscious of an overwhelming sense of . . . relief? He looked at Troy, wondering if the brush with certain discovery had shaken her composure.

She was smiling at him.

"The Lincoln Memorial," she whispered. "Tomorrow—I mean, today—around two in the afternoon. Okay?"

Instead of replying, Dallas leaned farther out and let his gaze follow the rope upward to where it disappeared over the edge of the roof. Then he looked back at the most unusual cat burglar he was ever likely to encounter. "The Lincoln Memorial. At two," he murmured, defeated.

"Leave the window open about an inch," she instructed efficiently. "And the drapes as well. See you tomorrow." Then she began to move up the rope hand over hand, her feet walking up the wall as easily as if it had been a floor.

Ten minutes later Dallas was back in his bed-room. He found himself staring at a rolled-up painting and a flashlight. Muttering to himself, he thrust both under his pillows, taking care not to press down on them when he tossed his robe aside and got into bed. He turned off the lamp on his nightstand and lay back, staring up into darkness. And he said only one more word, a word that seemed to his bewildered mind to sum up exactly how he felt about the entire situation.

"Hell."

Some time later, and two miles away from the isolated house she'd left behind her, Troy climbed into a waiting helicopter. She strapped herself in and then donned headphones to talk to the pilot over the roar of the aircraft as it lifted off.

"Home, James," she said cheerfully.

"I don't see the painting." It was a bear-rumble of a voice, exactly suited to the broad, stolid face of the middle-aged man at the controls.

Troy finally allowed the evening's accumulated giggles to escape. "It's being delivered, Jamie. Tomorrow at the Lincoln Memorial."

A grunt was Jamie's only response until the helicopter was well on its way to an airstrip near a fashionable suburb of Washington, D.C. When he did speak, the bear-rumble voice was amused, affectionate, and rueful. "You've found another stray, eh?"

Swallowing another giggle, Troy said casually, "I'd hardly call Dallas Cameron a stray. Would you?"

The helicopter dipped slightly at an ungentle jerk on the controls. Jamie's incredulous eyes stabbed at her across the dimly lit cockpit. "Dallas Cameron?" he asked faintly.

"Uh-huh."

"Scrupulously legal Dallas Cameron?"

"The very same."

"The one they call 'Ace' to his face and 'Genghis Khan' behind his back?"

"Yep."

"Oh, God."

TWO

DALLAS CAMERON HAD lived in Washington for nearly two months now. He'd moved his main office from the heart of the Silicon Valley in California to D.C. slightly more than six months ago, and had spent those first few months commuting between the two offices. Now the West Coast office was in capable hands, and Dallas had chosen to remain in the East.

He'd discovered that he enjoyed the hectic pace of life in the nation's capital, enjoyed being surrounded by historic sights and the multilingual, multinational people who lived and worked there. His house was out of the hands of decorators now and was beginning to feel like a home to him, and he'd already landed a rather substantial contract with a certain government department to supply electronic components for aircraft and spacecraft.

Now, sitting on the wide steps of the Lincoln Memorial, Dallas wondered dispassionately what the odds were against his being in the most policed city in the country with a stolen painting in his hands and not getting caught.

"Idiot," he muttered to himself, watching his words assume a frosty shape in the cold air and then dropping his gaze to the cardboard tube held in his gloved hands. He asked himself if he was here because he'd believed Troy's story about the painting, or simply because he wanted very badly to see her again, in broad daylight this time, without the sense of unreality he'd felt during last night's meeting.

He knew the right answer.

Thoughtfully Dallas gazed out across the long pool separating the Lincoln Memorial and Washington Monument, his eyes following the string of Japanese cherry trees lining the

Reflecting Pool. Their limbs were bare now, not yet ready to flower into the beautiful blossoms that would draw the eyes of tourists and natives alike. Lovely blossoms.

What color were her eyes? And her hair? How old was she? And how, for God's sake, had she stumbled onto her extremely odd occupation? Did she ever, he wondered, steal paintings from their rightful owners?

Uneasily Dallas shifted slightly, the movement due not to the cold marble beneath him but to uncertain thoughts.

Although no one in his or her right mind would ever call Dallas naive, more than one of his less scrupulous business associates had accused him of being unworldly in certain views and judgments. To Dallas there was right and there was wrong, and a man took his stand on both. He could be utterly ruthless in business, but Dallas Cameron would never step outside the morality he'd established for himself. He didn't break laws, and he didn't break people; there were no footprints on other backs from Dallas's climb to the top. Not many successful businessmen of thirty-six could claim that they had never hurt another human being through business practices, intentionally or not; Dallas, had he been asked, could say just that with absolute honesty.

There *had* been hurt that he realized he was responsible for at least in part in his personal—which was to say romantic—life. But those hurts had been unintentional and were, even now, deeply regretted. That was a major reason why Dallas, as the saying went, played the field. Dallas wanted no scalps dangling from his belt.

Still, a man could control certain aspects of his life, he believed. A man made choices. He decided whether or not to abuse alcohol and drugs. He chose a certain life-style. He obeyed laws or broke them. He treated people with honor or he didn't. And sometimes he set himself a moral code he believed in, and he lived within it.

Troy. Whether her intentions sprang from the best or worst of motives, she nonetheless broke the law. Stealing, for whatever reason, was legally and morally *wrong*.

Dallas heard himself laugh shortly.

"That's odd: you laughed, but you look as if you were contemplating throwing yourself into the Reflecting Pool."

The voice was cheerful, a breath of spring on a winter day, and before Dallas could rise, she was sitting on the step beside him. He half turned, ridiculously eager to see Troy in the honest light of day. And his first thought was that the shadows of last night had cheated him. Badly.

She was smaller, for one thing; not much over five feet tall, he guessed. She was wearing a sheepskin jacket over a black turtleneck sweater and faded jeans, her small feet encased in scuffed desert boots. Her face was as delicately lovely as he remembered, her smooth ivory complexion untouched by freckles and radiating a rare translucence. Her large eyes were tilted at the outer ends in a catlike manner, and were green with gold flecks. Or...gold with green flecks. Odd; he wasn't sure which.

Her brows, too, were slanted, giving her an uncanny air of mystery. Well-molded cheekbones, a delicately straight nose, a firm jaw and chin, a long slender neck—and a beautiful mouth curved with pure laughter. And she was a redhead.

Dallas didn't doubt for a moment that Troy was a true redhead. Her vivid hair was the color of a flame, the color women and their hairdressers strove for in vain because it could never come out of a bottle. Falling to just below her shoulder blades, her hair was styled simply; parted in the center, it was thick and slightly wavy, curling under at the ends. And it shone like burnished bronze, Dallas thought, looking vibrantly alive even in winter's weak sunshine.

"Finished with the inventory?"

Dallas blinked and tried to concentrate enough to string a few words together that made reasonable sense. She wasn't, he realized, either annoyed or disturbed by his scrutiny. If anything, she was simply amused. He looked into the strangely shifting colors of her eyes and found no conceit there, not even an awareness of her own beauty.

Impossible, he told himself. She couldn't possibly not *know*....

"Sorry," he muttered, unable to stop staring.

Troy leaned back against the step behind her, resting her weight on her elbow. "Did you know that this memorial is made of Colorado marble?" she asked conversationally. "It has thirty-six Doric columns, which represent the number of states in the Union when Lincoln was killed."

She wore no rings, he noticed, and her hands

were slender with long, clever fingers and unpolished nails that were neat ovals. "No," he said finally. "I didn't know that."

Troy nodded toward the pool and the Washington Monument. "Did you know that the monument was dedicated in 1885 and designed by Robert Mills?"

"No." Dallas frowned suddenly. "Why're you making like a tour guide?"

Her green-gold/gold-green eyes laughed at him. "I had to say something. You sure weren't holding up your end of the conversation."

To his surprise and intense annoyance Dallas felt himself flushing for the first time in years. "Sorry," he repeated stiffly.

Troy waved a hand in another of those oddly controlled yet expressive gestures. "Forget it. By the way—did your host rather casually ask you this morning if you'd ever tried to crack a safe?"

A smile tugging at his mouth, Dallas said, "You're a smart lady, aren't you? As a matter of fact, John did. I've never claimed to be an actor, but I must have shown the proper amount of bewildered surprise, since he dropped the subject immediately."

"How'd you get the painting out?" Troy asked, her own smile showing even white teeth and one elusive dimple.

Fascinated by the dimple, Dallas almost forgot to answer. "Under my coat." He handed her the cardboard tube suddenly. "Here—take the damn thing. I've been looking over my shoulder ever since I left John's house this morning."

"Thinking he'd come after you?" Troy asked dryly, accepting the painting.

"No," Dallas told her. "Thinking about all the police in this city."

"I would have confessed if they'd nabbed you," she said solemnly.

Dallas wasn't amused. He was, in fact, more disturbed than he could ever remember being in his life. He had a flashing vision of endless nights haunted by dreams of beautiful redheaded cat burglars, and winced. "Dammit," he swore softly, yet roughly. "Why'd I have to walk in on you last night?"

The smile left her face but not her eyes; the smile there was tiny and uncomfortably perceptive. "Scrupulously legal Dallas Cameron," she murmured.

He looked at her steadily. "Stealing is wrong."

"Even for the right reasons?"

Disregarding that, Dallas said, "The rightful owner should have gone to the police. Then John would be behind bars, where he belongs."

Troy shook her head slightly. "He did go to the police." The smile had not left her eyes; it seemed to belong there as an innate, permanent thing. "But do you know how many art objects are stolen every year? The police don't even know for sure, because private collectors of stolen paintings sometimes steal from each other, and the thefts, of course, go unreported. Thefts from museums and legitimate collectors number in the hundreds— even thousands—each year. Most are transported out of the countries they were stolen in. Interpol does its best, and its best is very, very good. But sometimes there are no clues, and the art objects never surface."

Interested in spite of himself, Dallas asked, "Is that what happened in this case?"

"More or less." Troy looked at him thoughtfully for a moment, then went on calmly. "When the collector got in touch with me, I called my contact at Interpol in Paris. He told me that they had no leads, either on the thief or the painting, and that they didn't recognize the thief's M.O.—modus operandi; I'm sure you recognize the term from cop and detective shows on television. Anyway, he told me to have at it. And wished me well."

Dallas felt floored—and looked it. "You mean, he actually *told* you to try and steal the painting?"

"He told me to *recover* it if I could." For the first time there was the faintest hint of steel beneath Troy's easy manner. And the eyes that looked at Dallas, still containing their smile, were suddenly more green than gold. "Breaking as few laws as possible along the way." The last was said with a touch of sarcasm.

Stubbornly, perhaps suicidally, Dallas kept digging. "You're telling me that an officer of an international police organization gave you his approval to break into a private home and steal something?"

Troy watched him for a moment, as if deciding whether or not to respond to his question. One corner of her mouth was lifted in a crooked half-smile that was, any of her friends could have warned Dallas, a distant rumble of thunder before a violent storm. The tiny smile still glinted within her definitely green eyes. She sat up abruptly, holding the painting negligently in one hand. "Mr. Cameron—"

"Dallas," he corrected automatically, and the look in her eyes then made him feel suddenly small and oddly in the wrong.

"Mr. Cameron," she repeated with absolutely no inflection in her voice. "Like many redheads, I have hell's own temper. I also believe that my work is necessary, and I enjoy it. And if that isn't enough for you, then listen to this: You walked in last night on—in your own interpretation—a crime. If it'll make you feel better, go to the police. But don't preach at me. I'm a second-story woman; I can live with that. You don't have to."

Dallas looked away from the compelling green of her eyes. He saw a massively built man stumping determinedly up the steps to their right and several steps below them, the intense expression of a tourist on his broad face. But Dallas paid little attention to the man. Instead, he focused on the only part of her level speech that he could respond to. "Second-story woman?"

"Another term for cat burglar," she said dryly.

"Shhhh!" he hissed as the tourist drew level with them, then moved on up the steps.

"Why not expose me to the world?" Troy asked him coolly. "This is your chance, Mr. Cameron. Look—there's a cop. Will you flag him down, or shall I?"

Dallas turned his head to glare at her; oddly she was smiling again, and her eyes were shifting in color from green to gold. "Dammit," Dallas muttered, feeling a furious rage because the expletive wasn't strong enough.

"Well?" she taunted softly.

He reached out suddenly, one gloved hand curving around the back of her neck and pulling her toward him with a jerk that should have unbalanced her. But it didn't. When his lips found hers, Dallas felt a moment of tension in her, a moment during which, he realized dimly, she was on the edge of exploding into action with the ferocity of a wildcat. Then she relaxed, her lips softening and warming beneath his. But she made no effort to touch him of her own volition.

Dallas kissed her as if he would pull something from deep within her and make it his own. He kissed her with the fury and gentleness of a man who sought something he couldn't put a name to, something too powerful to fight and too elusive to understand. And when he finally drew back, his dark blue eyes were almost black, and his breath came harshly.

"Does that answer your question?" he rasped.

Troy leaned back slowly away from him, her own eyes dark gold and her breathing quick. She looked at him steadily as his hand fell away from her neck, no pretense in her eyes of not understanding him. "It's impossible," she told him quietly, her voice husky. "You must see that. I'm a thief. For whatever reason, in your eyes I'm a thief. And I won't stop being what I am."

"Troy—"

"Thinking of reforming me?" In control again, her steady gaze was both rueful and ironical. "That only happens in bad novels and worse movies. Why should I give up something I *feel* is right just because you—a virtual stranger—think it's wrong?"

His eyes were restless, impatient. "Look, if you had a legitimate career, I wouldn't think of asking you to give it up, but—"

"As it happens," she interrupted calmly, "I do

have a legitimate career. I develop and set up security systems for people. Isn't that funny?"

"For God's sake," Dallas said blankly.

Troy watched his astonishment for a moment, then spoke again. "I don't know exactly what you have in mind, Mr. Cameron—"

"Dallas!" he exploded. "Dammit to hell, call me Dallas!"

She compromised: she didn't call him anything. "—but whatever you have in mind wouldn't work. You won't abandon your scruples, and I don't have any."

"Will you stop waving that at me like a banner of pride?" he demanded wrathfully. "It's nothing to brag about."

Troy sighed, beginning to be honestly amused. "You know, I've run head-on into some moral walls in my time, but yours rivals the Great Wall of China. And though it'd probably be quite interesting to knock a few blocks out of the thing, I just don't have the patience. You'll have to look somewhere else for your fling."

"That wasn't what I had in mind," he told her irritably. "And what makes you so damn sure it's *my* wall that needs to come tumbling down?"

"Not tumbling down. It just needs a few blocks knocked out of it to let the fresh air in."

Dallas strove with himself. "What about your wall?"

"Don't have one. Just lots of wide open spaces." She smiled easily. "It's called being broad-minded."

"It's called being a thief," he snapped.

Troy shrugged. "Call a spade a spade. Doesn't bother me."

Dallas reached desperately for an argument to combat her calm certainty. "You're paid money to steal. You *gain* from theft. Don't you see how wrong that is?"

After a moment Troy said neutrally, "And if I didn't gain? Would that make it more acceptable?"

"Hell—I—maybe. I don't know. It's a moot point anyway. You were *hired* to steal that painting from John. What he did by hiring someone else to steal it for him doesn't excuse what you did. Two wrongs don't make a right, dammit."

Troy would have laughed at the cliché, except that she could hear the struggle in his deep voice. She kept her own voice level. "In this case, at least, two wrongs do make a right. John was punished by the loss of his money as well as the painting, and Interpol will keep an eye on him from now on; not a thing could be proved against him in court—"

"It could have if you hadn't stolen the evidence."

"There were no grounds for a search warrant," she said flatly. "Remember the law? The police couldn't get inside his house to *find* the evidence. Suspicion isn't enough."

Balked, Dallas tried again. "What about the thief John hired? He gets off."

"Only for the moment." Troy smiled slightly. "I had to track him down in order to find out who'd hired him; Interpol now has a nice little eight-by-ten glossy of him. And since I'm reasonably sure he pulled off that jewel heist in London last week, I'm sure they'll get him."

Dallas stared at her silently.

"All out of arguments?" she asked dryly.

"No. It's wrong to steal. It's wrong to gain by stealing."

Troy sighed. "Look, never mind. You go your way and I'll go mine, okay, pal? Life's too short for this kind of a debate."

"I can't walk away," he said, his voice grating softly.

Troy fought to ignore the leap of her heart. "It's the novelty, don't you see that? You've never met a cat burglar before—much less a *woman* cat burglar."

"So?"

"So it'll pass. And you'll be glad you didn't try to reform a hardened criminal."

Dallas made a slight, almost unconscious gesture, as if to sweep her last word into oblivion. "It won't pass. And I'm not through trying." His blue eyes bored into hers. "I want to know who you are, where you live, whether you like animals. I want to know your favorite colors and your favorite foods, and if you play tennis or bridge. I want to know where you were born and grew up, where you went to school, and who cleans your teeth.

"I can find that out, Troy. No life leaves no traces. If I don't learn you *from* you, then I'll hire detectives—every detective in the damn city if that's what it takes—and I'll find out everything I want to know about you."

Troy's face was very still, the smile in her eyes briefly extinguished. But then it surfaced again.

"You know," she said slowly, "I'm...almost... tempted to call you on that."

"It's not a bluff," he warned evenly.

"Why?" she asked. "Why so determined?"

"You know. You're woman enough to know."

She tamed the leap of her heart again. "You're asking for trouble," she warned in turn. "I honestly don't believe that two people as different as you and I could ever find common ground. And I'm past the age of believing that chemistry can form the basis of anything except experiments in a laboratory."

Dallas ignored that. "It's your choice. Either you let me find out about you in the...acceptable way, or else you force me to employ other methods."

"What do you expect to find out?" she asked, suddenly curious. "That I was twisted by heredity and environment and turned into a criminal? That I lead a life of shadows, a life filled with shady meetings and surreptitious phone calls? That I live in a house filled with stolen loot and cringe whenever a police officer passes?"

"I want to find out what's there," Dallas said flatly.

Troy looked at him for a long moment. Then she shrugged. "All right. If you're so damn determined to look into the nooks and crannies of my life, feel free. Believe it or not, I've nothing to hide."

Dallas almost relaxed. "Fine. Where do I pick you up for dinner tonight?"

She bit back a laugh. "Arrogant, aren't you? Give you an inch and you run away with it."

"You didn't answer the question."

"Was that a question? It sounded like a command. If I must have a sparring partner, you'd better know the rules. And rule number one is that I won't be ordered around. Period."

"Pardon me. Would you please have dinner with me tonight?"

"No."

"Dammit!"

Dryly Troy said, "Look, last night was a long one, and it didn't end for me after I left you. In fact, I haven't been to bed. I intend to go home and have a nice nap, after which I'll call the collector in Paris. Then I plan to fall back into bed and sleep all night."

Dallas controlled himself. "Tomorrow night

then?" He only just remembered to make it a question.

"I'm giving a party. You're welcome to come: the address is Three-oh-nine Oak Street. It starts at eight or thereabouts. Formal." When Dallas looked at her suspiciously, she shook her head slightly. "I'm not giving a phony address: I don't lie. Funny little quirk of mine."

He finally nodded. "All right."

"Don't expect to meet the cream of thieving society," she warned lightly. "You're more likely to see diplomats, politicians. Army and arty types, maybe a few senators or congressmen...judges. I'm a democratic hostess."

When he recovered from that, Dallas said wryly, "Maybe I'd better ask something before I come to your party."

"Ask away."

"Among the distinguished types mentioned, there isn't a husband, is there?"

"Scores of them. But none belonging to me."

"You're not married?"

"Someone's going to have to get me pregnant first," she said sweetly.

"I'll remember that," he shot back calmly.

Troy remained seated while he rose to his feet, thinking that she was going to regret this. As a sparring partner, he lacked nothing; but sparring partners didn't exactly make for comfortable relationships—and Troy found all the excitement she needed in her work.

"Eight," he said, looking down at her.

"Or thereabouts," she responded easily.

He kept looking down at her. "You haven't called me by my name yet," he noted neutrally.

"Is that a prerequisite to being investigated?" she asked dryly.

"Troy."

She was never able afterward to explain to herself what it was about his voice that got to her. It might have been the yearning note that, she was certain, echoed only in her imagination. It might have been that no one else had ever said her name in quite that way. Whatever it was, it got to her.

"Okay. I'll see you around eight—Dallas."

A smile curved his mouth, something warm kindling in his dark blue eyes. "I'll see you tomorrow night, Troy." Then he turned and made his way down the steps.

As Troy watched his lean figure disappear into

the distance the big man who'd been waiting, silent and watchful, among the Doric columns at the top of the steps came down to join her. He sat beside her, joining her in looking after the man who'd just left.

"You walked past us very pointedly," she observed absently.

"You were smiling your dangerous smile," the big man explained in a voice that sounded like an angry bear at the bottom of a deep well. "I thought I'd better pass by to remind you not to light into Cameron."

"I nearly did, Jamie," she said ruefully. "He was needling me about stealing being wrong."

Jamie looked at her curiously. "Even after you explained that you don't gain by it?"

Troy slid a look at her big companion. "Yes, well—I didn't exactly tell him about that."

"Why not?"

"I don't know. Yes—I do know. He was so damn complacent about his belief and so utterly unwilling to listen to mine. To *hear* mine. I think he wants to reform me, if you please. And I have a terrible suspicion that he's going to try and blame my unlawful ways on heredity and/or environment. He probably thinks my father was a Skid Row bum and my mother a hooker."

Jamie hid a smile at her disgusted tone. "You've met others who wanted to place your delicate feet on the straight and narrow," he said mildly.

"I know. But dammit, he makes me mad."

"Then tell him the truth."

"That he makes me mad? He knows that."

"No, *mon enfant*—tell him about yourself."

"He wouldn't believe me."

"Show him."

"That's his idea." Troy sighed, then muttered abruptly. "I think I own stock in his company."

Jamie burst out laughing at the sudden astonishment in her voice, his own tone even more of a bear-rumble in amusement. "Well, he left calmly enough, at any rate. You must have said something to placate him."

"I invited him to my party," Troy said woefully.

Remembering the kiss he'd seen, Jamie said rather carefully, "Was that wise, *chérie*?"

"No." She sighed. "It wasn't a bit wise. But he said that either he'd find out about me *from* me, or else he'd hire detectives. And I don't think he was bluffing, Jamie."

"May I ask why he's so determined?"

Troy looked at him with a comical mixture of caution and amusement. "Well, don't go all stuffy and protective, but I'm reasonably sure he has designs on my virtue."

Jamie, the memory of that kiss strong, was more than reasonably sure. He was certain. "I promised your father I'd look after you, *mon enfant*."

"You've taught me to look after myself," she reminded.

"True. And you're over twenty-one. But be careful. Cameron strikes me as being an honest man, but he's not known for his fidelity."

Troy got to her feet, holding the almost-forgotten painting securely. "Fidelity doesn't interest me, Jamie. I'm not ready to settle down."

Jamie rose more slowly, his face concerned as he looked down at her. "You've never been in love, *chérie*. But when you fall, you'll fall hard. I just don't want to see you hurt."

The talents of a genuinely great actress must have been passed down to Troy; her laugh sounded sure and heart-whole even to herself. "Love? Jamie, Dallas Cameron thinks I'm a thief, and nothing's going to change his opinion. And I could never fall in love with a man who thought me immoral. It just isn't possible." She started down the steps confidently.

"Besides, as soon as the novelty wears off, he'll be gone."

Moving after her, Jamie muttered, "Uh-huh. When pigs grow wings and hell freezes over."

If Troy heard him, she gave no sign.

The house on Oak Street was nestled in among the towering trees that had given the street its name. It was a tall and stately house, a generation older than Troy, and it boasted some thirty rooms. The mansion—a well-cared-for Colonial—was beautiful.

When Troy briskly entered the house through the front door, Bryce was there to take her jacket, as always just a moment too late to open the door for her as he thought proper. Troy hid a grin at the slight crack in his butlerly composure, silently admonishing herself, as always, that she really should stop bolting into the house and upsetting the poor man.

"Three messages, Miss Troy," he announced in his clipped British accent, holding the much used and despised (by him) sheepskin jacket as though it were a mink coat. "The French gentleman called again and asked that you return his call at your convenience."

"Uh-huh."

"Mr. Elliot called to inform you that he is bringing the ingredients for his—punch—to the gathering tomorrow night."

Bryce said *punch* as if it were a blow from a fist rather than a drink, Troy thought in amusement. She smothered a yawn behind one hand, the exhaustion of too many hours without sleep beginning to catch up with her. "Fine. And the third message?"

"A gentleman," Bryce said, his emphasis proclaiming that he had his doubts about the noun, "called and asked if Troy lived here. Then he demanded to know your last name."

"You hung up on him, of course?" Troy murmured, thinking that Dallas had worked fast to get her unlisted number. How on earth had he managed?

"Of course." The butler unbent enough to say

somewhat sternly, "Mrs. Miller is preparing something light for your dinner, Miss Troy. I would suggest that you lie down for a few hours before the meal."

Amused, Troy said, "I'm way ahead of you, Bryce."

Ten minutes later Troy had stripped and slid between cool sheets in her French Provincial bedroom. Just as she was relaxing into sleep, a sudden thought made her sit up and reach for the phone on her nightstand. She placed a call, asked one brief question, listened to the answer, then expressed her thanks and hung up.

Lying back on the pillows, she thought with drowsy irritation, *Damn, I do own stock in his company!*

THREE

THE ALCOVE AT the top of the stairs was a perfect place from which to observe comings and goings, and Troy used it for just that. None of her guests would expect her until they saw her: it was neither lack of punctuality nor any desire for theatrics that made her invariably late for even her own parties, but merely a life filled to overflowing with things to be done. As it was, she'd only finished getting ready five minutes before, and the party had been in full swing for almost an hour.

So she paused in the alcove, shielded by shadows from the eyes of her guests below as she took a moment to catch her breath and gaze down on the cream of several different crops of Washington society. The military was represented in all of its branches and most of its ranks; the occasional wafting upward of foreign words and phrases indicated the presence of members of the diplomatic corps: strident "discussions" of the economy hinted at government representatives; glittering jewels and evening dresses announced fashionable society.

It was a sight to gladden the heart of any hostess, but Troy merely noted the guests with cursory interest. Familiar faces all, and though she was always glad to see friends, she was looking for a particular face at the moment.

And there he was.

Troy felt her heart leap, and fiercely steadied it. Of course, he'd come; the man was determined if nothing else. Shatteringly handsome in a black dinner jacket, he strode through the huge sitting room, clearly visible to her through the archway across from the stairs.

He moved like a cat, she thought vaguely, like a slightly aloof and innately arrogant Siamese. And the crowd that was filled with important people, with world movers and shakers, seemed automatically to give way before him in an unconscious acceptance of superiority.

Troy frowned at that. Not even her dearest friends would have ventured to call her pliant or self-effacing, and when two arrogant and stubborn personalities met head-on...

Now she was frowning at herself. Idiot, she thought. Dallas Cameron would very shortly lose interest in a thief met in the night, so there was really no need for this unsatisfactory comparison of personalities. Besides, what they didn't have in common would fill volumes, and she'd probably never see him again after tonight.

Unconsciously biting her lower lip, Troy continued to watch as he progressed through the crowded sitting room and into the vast entrance hall below her. She'd always thought that no man was ever as handsome as he could be unless in uniform, but Dallas Cameron, she acknowledged silently, didn't need the gilding. He overpowered and overshadowed every other man here tonight, even the silver-haired judge commonly considered the sexiest man in the city.

Troy smoothed unexpectedly nervous hands

down her thighs, studying his cat-footed, Indian-file walk and noting, even at this distance, that his blue eyes were restlessly searching the crowd of faces. She knew who he was looking for, and a sudden tugging in the pit of her stomach weakened her composure momentarily.

But then Troy squared her shoulders and stepped determinedly out of the alcove. He was just a man, dammit, no more and no less. Just a man, and no threat to her peace. Just a flesh-and-blood man.

With a face that had haunted her dreams...

In spite of Troy's light warning, Dallas hadn't expected the definitely democratic mix of types at her party. In the hour he'd been here, he had already spoken to a general, two colonels, a judge, a senator, two congressmen, a society deb, three business moguls he knew well, a pro quarterback, three artists, and a very famous popular singer.

He also hadn't expected this house, although he'd driven past it twice the day before, feeling a strong sense of disbelief. And his disbelief had grown with every brief conversation held here tonight; he had smoothly and subtly questioned everyone he met about his hostess.

In a city where scandal and gossip ran rampant, and backstabbing—verbal or otherwise— was commonplace, Troy's reputation appeared to be inviolate.

She had apparently collected a variety of nicknames: Kat, Red, Honey, T.B., Tiny, and—inexplicably to Dallas—Blaze. And Tom Elliot, the popular singer and heartthrob whose function at the party seemed to be guarding a punchbowl, referred cheerfully to her as Blondie. After the comic strip? he wondered.

Dallas tried and failed to reconcile these new versions of the woman with his own ideas. Who was she? *What* was she, for heaven's sake?

Wandering out into the entrance hall, he continued to wonder where she was. He searched unfamiliar faces, looking for gold-green/green-gold eyes and flaming hair. (Blaze! Of course! he thought.) And then he saw her descending the stairs, and rational thought fled.

Flaming coppery hair was piled high on her head, adding a new and disconcerting dignity, and she moved like a queen. Her gown was stark black with a plunging V-neckline, and it clung to her body with more affection than a second skin. Her eyes were green-flecked gold tonight, emphasized by lightly shadowing makeup...and they were vividly alive. There were diamonds around her throat and circling one wrist; high heels added inches and still more dignity to an innate sinuous grace that was riveting.

Dallas swallowed the remainder of his drink and automatically set it on the tray of a passing maid.

Troy spoke lightly and casually as she reached the bottom step, refusing to allow the intensity in his eyes to disturb her. "Hello. Enjoying the party?"

Dallas found that he had to clear his throat before words would emerge. "I am now," he told her huskily.

Unlike most redheads Troy wasn't a blushing woman, but she felt heat sweep up her throat. Leaning an elbow on the banister, she strove for blasé acceptance of the compliment. "How sweet," she murmured languidly, long lashes dropping to veil her eyes in a perfect imitation of a bored society deb.

Laughter abruptly lit his blue eyes. "You do that very well," he noted approvingly. "Have you tried it on the quarterback?"

The society deb vanished and Troy fought to hide a grin. "You mean, Rick? Is he moping again?"

"If by moping you mean, is he boring everyone silly with his hangdog look and monologues about you, the answer is yes. How many other callow youths will I find entangled in your web, Miss Bennett?"

"Scores of them," she answered solemnly. "I collect them, you see." Then, abruptly serious, she said, "His team had a losing season, poor kid, so he's feeling generally morose."

Testing her reaction, Dallas murmured, "He seems to be suffering more under the weight of unrequited love at the moment."

Gazing at him with that disquieting little smile in her remarkable eyes, Troy shook her head slightly. "Trying to see me as coldhearted as well as a thief, Cameron?"

"And if I were?"

"Then you will." A crooked smile lifted one corner of her mouth and flashed an elusive dimple.

"Your opinions are your own; I'm not responsible for them."

For some reason Dallas couldn't let the subject drop. And the memory of the young quarterback's besotted expression when he spoke of Troy roused something deep within Dallas from a peaceful sleep. "That kid's in love with you," he said flatly, all teasing and testing over.

Troy started to step past him, but halted to stare down at the hand encircling her wrist. Her eyes lifted slowly to lock with his, and the green fire in hers should have warned him.

It really should have.

"Mr. Cameron," she said in a deceptively mild voice. "You seem to be under the mistaken impression that I give a damn what you think. Banish it. And please try to remember that you're a guest under my roof."

"I've had a look at what's under this roof," he said roughly, still clasping her wrist, "and I can't help but wonder how you came to—uh—acquire the art treasures I've seen."

"Why, Mr. Cameron, you mean, you don't know?" With a sudden and unexpectedly powerful twist, she freed her wrist. Stepping past him, she added smoothly over her shoulder, "I stole them, of course."

Dallas could have kicked himself for provoking her, wondering with a confused mixture of anger and bewilderment why he couldn't seem to stop himself from constantly digging. He watched her move away from him, noting the immediate smiles her presence caused, and the sleeping beast, roused by the callow youth's smitten eyes, lunged on its chain.

He wanted to—had to—understand her. Never in his life had a woman ignited his body and mind the way Troy did. Never before had primitive urges tormented him awake and asleep. And never before had the two sides of his own nature, the ruthless and the sensitive, been so at odds with each other.

He had always found a delicate balance within himself. Ruthless up to a point, his sensitivity always announced itself and restrained him from injuring another or breaking his own moral code. But his ruthless side was clamoring now, demanding with a voice out of the caves of man's distant past. And the demand was for possession.

Still and silent, watching her from the bottom

of the stairs, Dallas fought an inner battle that was no less violent for its absence of sound. The emotions welling up inside of him were unfamiliar, yet he understood them. And in that moment he realized for the first time in his life the meaning of the word *obsession*.

He was well on his way to being obsessed with Troy Bennett.

Troy deliberately and consciously lost track of Dallas Cameron. She moved among her guests, chatting and laughing, automatically performing the duties of a hostess even while inwardly seething.

How dare he judge her? How *dare* he? Damn the man! And to imply that she had callously ignored poor Rick's open adoration! Didn't he realize that she was well aware of the crush, and was handling it the best way she knew by treating it lightly?

She clamped a lid on her temper, and it spoke volumes for her self-control that no one she talked to realized that she was absolutely furious.

After two hours, however, with the party still in

full swing, the strain of smiling and talking lightly began to wear on Troy. Refusing to search for his face in the crowd—had he left?—she slipped away and found the library thankfully empty of guests.

Wandering over to the big leather chair that had been her father's, Troy rested her hands on the high back and overcame an impulse to throw something. Then inexplicably she felt tears rise in her eyes. She was suddenly tired clear down to her bones. It all seemed so empty: the house her parents had loved, the round of parties she was expected to attend, the once heady excitement of recovering stolen property.

She wondered absently if it would have made a difference if she'd told Dallas that she was a licensed private investigator or that insurance companies often hired her to investigate thefts of art objects.

No. He had met a thief in the night, and probably nothing would alter that crucial negative first impression.

Idiot. She was just tired, that was all. How many years had it been since she'd last taken a real vacation? Too many. Yes, she was just tired.

But Troy recognized it was more than that. Brooding silently over the vagaries of fate, she heard the library door close softly, and knew who would be there even before she looked up.

He was leaning back against the door, staring across the softly lighted room at her. There was something in his gaze, a curiously beaten expression that tugged at her, and Troy wondered what it meant.

"More taunting?" she asked, her voice level.

"No." He shook his head slightly, adding quietly, "I've come to apologize."

"It doesn't matter."

"It does."

With a tremendous effort Troy managed to keep her voice impersonal. "You and I are like two flints, Cameron—bound to strike sparks off each other."

Slowly he said, "Sparks can start a fire that warms."

"Or consumes." She gazed at him steadily. "I've never put much faith in pretty speeches or euphemistic terms, Cameron, so tell me now exactly what you want of me."

"I want to know you," he answered immediately.

Troy laughed shortly. "Know me how? As a novelty?"

"No, dammit." Dallas pushed himself away from the door and crossed the room to stand beside her. "You're a fascinating woman, Troy Bennett. And I'm very much afraid that you've become an obsession with me."

Troy felt a lump in her throat, felt her heart pounding in a suddenly uneven rhythm, and looked down at her hands in an attempt to ignore the intense blue of his eyes. "Why?" she murmured, not sure she wanted to hear his answer.

Dimly, the sound muffled by walls and shelves of books, the strains of a love song came from the sitting room as the musicians returned from their break. Dallas turned his head slightly, listening, then looked back at her. Ignoring her question, he asked a soft one of his own. "Dance with me?"

Troy looked up at him slowly, disturbed by his eyes, by his oddly taut face, by his request. "I don't think—"

"Dance with me." He reached for her hand,

holding it firmly as he stepped back and drew her away from the chair. "Let me hold you."

It was the last husky plea that weakened her defenses, and Troy went into his arms silently. Stiff, wary, she felt his breath softly stirring the tendrils of hair at her temple and wondered at the fluttering in her belly.

You've danced with princes, she reminded herself in confusion. With princes and sheikhs, presidents and movie stars. With men who moved the world through their actions.

Why did this man, and only this man, shake her?

He held her as closely as possible without using force, aware of her resistance. Unhurriedly he lifted both her hands to his neck, dropping his own to her waist and easily spanning its tiny girth. Inch by inch, with only a gentle pressure, he drew her even closer.

The movement was so insidious, so perfectly timed with the slow steps of their dance, that Troy became aware of the lessening distance between them only when she felt her breasts brush his dinner jacket. Her breath caught in her throat with a gasp, the silky slide of her dress over the bare flesh it covered intensified by the rough material of his jacket. She wanted to draw away, but there was a weakness in her legs and in her soul, and she experienced a sudden need for a strength not her own.

She could feel his chin move against her temple, feel his chest rise and fall in a quickening rhythm. Without conscious volition her hands curled at the nape of his neck, her fingers losing themselves in his thick black hair. Breathless, suspended, she was dimly aware of their steps slowing even more until they were barely moving—outwardly.

Inwardly Troy felt violent surges, a red-hot movement of feelings and impulses she'd never experienced before. They tore through her body with the speed and devastation of a tornado, leaving weakness and bubbling desire in their aftermath. She wanted to break free of his embrace, but didn't have the strength; wanted to speak, but didn't have the breath.

God, oh, God, what was he doing to her?

She felt his hands slide up her back, scorching the flesh left bare by the low-cut gown, then drop suddenly to mold her hips and pull her hard against his lower body with abrupt impatience. What little breath she could command left her lips in a rush as the hard throbbing of his desire ignited her senses. Troy hid her face in his shoulder in an instinctive attempt to prevent him from seeing the helpless reaction.

"Troy..." His voice was deep, choked off somewhere in his throat, and his movements against her had become a primitive and sensuous dance needing no music.

She closed her eyes, breathing rapidly through parted lips, her fingers tangling fiercely in his hair. The kiss on the steps yesterday, she realized vaguely, had barely hinted that he could make her feel like this. He had stolen her breath then, but she sensed that he was stealing far, far more now. Her willpower. Her strength. Her soul. Herself....

The familiar and comforting library vanished; time ground to a halt. The bubble of need within her grew, expanded, until it filled her entire body. It throbbed in rhythm with his desire, demanding an end to a sweet and mindless torture. She felt his hands searching, exploring, creating a sensual friction with the silky material of her gown, and the bubble of desire filled with a hot rush of hunger.

"God," he whispered harshly, unevenly, "you're

not wearing a damn thing under this dress, are you?"

Troy heard the words, but the sensations in her body gripped and burned and refused to allow speech. She felt his lips moving down her cheek, along her jaw; felt the demanding heat of them stringing burning kisses down her throat. She lifted her head from his shoulder only to throw it back, the unconscious, provocative gesture allowing more scope for his explorations.

Mindless, eyes tightly closed, she stroked his silky hair helplessly and aided him in locking her body to his. Never in her life had she experienced such a burning hunger. She throbbed from head to toe, and she couldn't be close enough to him to satisfy the need to touch him.

There was no rational voice in her mind, no whisper of logical warnings. There was only this building, smothering feeling of reaching for something unknown to her. Reaching, and her body yearned to find it. Reaching, and the tension was unbearable. She heard a groan rumble from deep within Dallas's chest, and her senses spun dizzily.

And then, cutting suddenly through the layers of mindless desire and the silence of the library, the music, unheard by them for so long, now switched to a raucous, foot-tapping, jazz number.

Troy's eyes snapped open in shock, and her hands fell away from him. She felt his hands release her, saw his head lift and eyes as dazed as her own look down at her. And the shock of interruption merged with the sudden shock of awareness as she realized just how far she'd been willing to go with this virtual stranger.

Dancing, she thought dimly. We were just dancing....

She stepped back, feeling the rush of air cooling heated flesh and the rush of sanity replacing blind desire. One step, two, three; she backed away from him as if from a suddenly recognized devil. The big leather chair halted her retreat, and her hand fumbled for the touch of rich leather and reality.

"Troy..." He hadn't moved; he stood where she'd left him with every muscle tensed, and his face was white. A nerve pulsed erratically at one corner of his tightly held mouth. "You see why I have to know you?" His voice was uneven, harsh.

She swallowed hard, her nails leaving marks in the leather she was gripping. "Chemistry," she choked, the lump in her throat refusing to dissolve.

He took a sudden step toward her, the movement filled with the tension and unfulfilled hunger that was still throbbing in the air between them. "I've felt chemistry before," he bit out tautly. "But I've never felt anything like what just happened between us. And if you're honest, you'll admit the same thing."

Troy fought for some hold over her churning emotions, some stable surface to stand on. "What makes you so sure I haven't?" she challenged shakily. "I'm twenty-eight, Dallas, and I've seen a lot of the world. I could have had scores of lovers for all you know."

"Have you?" he asked very quietly.

She stared at him, wanting to lie but sensing dimly that it wouldn't matter to him. Driven by a curiosity she couldn't fight, she murmured, "What if I said yes?"

"It wouldn't matter," he answered flatly. "It wouldn't change anything, Troy."

"You'd just add promiscuity to my catalog of vices, I suppose?"

His head jerked slightly, denying the accusation. "No. If you told me you'd had scores of lovers, then I'd have to believe that you'd... cared...scores of times."

"Generous of you," she snapped softly, reaching for anger, for anything to combat the bewildered emotions she was feeling.

Dallas swore with a violence no less fierce in its quiet intensity. "Troy, I don't want to know how many lovers you've had. Don't tell me. All I want to know is that I'll be the only lover in your life...*now*."

Her body aching, Troy looked at him in silence. Then she shook her head. She didn't want an affair with Dallas, and she knew very well that nothing else would develop—could develop—out of their attraction. Opposites could attract, certainly, but rarely did they cling permanently. "I don't want a lover...*now*," she whispered.

"Troy—"

"Don't you understand?" Her voice was soft, driven. "When I see rain, I look for a rainbow. When I see thorns, I look for roses. But when I look at this—whatever it is—between us, I see only thorns and rain. All I see are the problems."

"If you'll just give it a chance—"

"And be left bleeding when it's over?" she interrupted, vulnerable, and not caring that he should see her vulnerability.

He took another step toward her. "You're looking at endings before beginnings," he told her huskily. "No one can say if it has to end—unless and until it does."

Troy attempted desperately to make him understand, afraid of what he could take from her if he tried. "A relationship with at least a possibility of...continuity is worth taking a chance on. But something that's impossible from the beginning—"

"It isn't impossible," he insisted softly.

Her smile was twisted. "Remember how we met? Remember your question not too long ago about how I 'acquired' the art treasures in this house? Your mistrust is a wall neither of us can break through."

"You don't have to be a thief," he snapped, and realized immediately and with a sinking sensation that he had unintentionally built the wall higher.

Her eyes were vividly green; she'd found the stable surface of anger to stand on. "Thief." She repeated his word with a soft and deadly emphasis. "You see? It's between us like an ocean, and I won't cross to your side, Dallas Cameron. I won't be taunted, and I won't be *reformed*. I am what I am, and you can't accept it. And I won't climb into bed with a man who calls me a thief." She drew a deep breath, finishing quietly, "So there's nothing to talk about, is there?"

Dallas gazed at her for a moment in silence. He fought the instincts urging him just to grab her and to hell with talk, leashing the violent emotions she had roused in him.

"Now, if you wouldn't mind leaving?" she suggested, wishing him gone because her anger had drained away and left behind it an urge to find a quiet corner and cry her eyes out. . . .

"But I would mind," he said abruptly. Before she could speak, he was going on unemotionally. "Thief. Yes, that's partly how I think of you. But if I've learned anything tonight, it's that you're a woman who . . . wears many hats. If I believed that you were *just* a thief, I wouldn't be standing here arguing with you; I'd be gone."

"Get to the point," she requested shortly, hanging on grimly to her composure.

Slowly he did. "I told you that I had to know

you, that you were becoming an obsession with me. You're like a—a picture not quite in focus, something my eyes are straining to see clearly." He took a deep breath. "Maybe you're right, and there's no future in it; but I have to believe that myself, and I don't. If you're so sure about us, Troy, then let me be sure too. Give me a chance to see you clearly."

"As a lover?" she inquired, her voice constricted.

Dallas hesitated, the curiously beaten expression appearing in his eyes again. "I hope . . . eventually. But as a woman first, as a person. I wouldn't ask you to climb into bed with a man who called you a thief, Troy."

Troy felt the breath catch in her throat, wondering dimly at the rough unsteadiness of his final sentence. What was he asking of her? And why couldn't she look away from his intensely blue eyes? She shook her head, not certain what she was denying.

"Please, Troy." His eyes held hers steadily. "Let me get to know you. No strings; no pressure, I promise you. And no taunting. I won't try to reform you. I won't rush you into a relationship you think we aren't ready for. I just want to see you . . . wearing all your hats."

Troy became suddenly aware that the band was playing another tune now, a love song, and the seductive, throbbing sound of it was undermining her resolution. She tore her gaze from his with a force that broke something inside of her, and confusion welled up again. "Damn you," she said very quietly.

"Troy." He took another step toward her, her name a plea, a caress, a demand on his lips.

She kept her face averted. "I don't want you in my life. You're a potential heartache walking around on two legs, and you're asking me to show you everything that I am."

"I won't hurt you." He was standing directly in front of her now.

Troy chuckled, only a breath of sound, and there was no amusement in it. "I don't believe you, you know. I've heard empty promises before, and that promise has all the earmarks of being empty." She looked up at him with eyes that seemed to be pure gold, and what he saw there nearly stopped his heart. "Keep your empty promises to yourself," she spit softly.

Dallas saw pain in her eyes, an old, half-healed scar. It shocked him oddly; until that moment he would have sworn that Troy had traveled lightly through her life, avoiding hurts. But the sight of her pain and vulnerability roused in him an anger at whomever had hurt her, and a fiercely protective emotion that he didn't try to define. He reached out to capture her resisting hands, holding them securely in his own.

"I don't make empty promises," he told her flatly. "Troy, all I'm asking is the chance to get to know you."

"And then what?" Molten gold burned up at him. "A roll in the hay because spring is in the air and you've never slept with a thief before?"

"Stop it." His hands tightened on hers. "Stop making what I feel for you sound cheap, because it isn't. I want you. Troy, because you're a beautiful, desirable woman. I want to be your lover, and at this moment I don't care if you've stolen the crown jewels of England."

Troy wanted to call him a liar, but the words wouldn't come. She looked down at the large, strong hands holding her own, and knew suddenly why she couldn't accuse him of lying. And she knew then that Dallas Cameron *was* going to hurt her, and hurt her badly.

Opposites could and did attract. The passion that was still a stubborn weakness in her body told her that. Opposites did attract...for a time. And she was drawn like a moth to the flame that would destroy it. Dallas had taken something from her, something she would never be able to recover. And when he left her one day...

"All right," she heard herself say quietly.

"Troy?" he breathed softly.

She met his gaze steadily. "You've got your chance. We'll get to know each other. But I won't let you interfere in my work." *Because it's all I'll have left when you've gone*, she added silently.

His chest moved with a sudden deep breath. "That's all I want—a chance," he said huskily.

Troy very gently pulled her hands from his grasp. "Now, since my guests will soon be drifting out, I should be there to say good night."

Dallas nodded. "I'll say good night now," he told her with an odd gentleness. "May I see you tomorrow?"

"I've got a busy week planned," she hedged.

He smiled a little. "Mind if I tag along?"

"What about your company? Shouldn't you be minding the store?"

"I haven't had a vacation in years; what's the use of being the boss if I can't take some time off?" he asked lightly.

Troy summoned a smile from somewhere. "All right then. But you'll probably be bored silly."

"I doubt that. What time?"

"Eight tomorrow morning."

His brows rose in faint surprise. "After a late night?"

"After a late night."

"I can take it if you can," he said wryly.

Troy watched him hesitate, observing that he had nearly bent his head to kiss her and wondering why he had apparently decided against it. But she didn't ask. Her eyes followed as he moved slowly to the door, absorbing the cat-footed grace that would rivet her gaze even in a crowd.

He half turned to look back at her. "Good night, Troy."

"Good night, Dallas."

She stood alone in the silent room for a long moment, her mind a blank. And when her own voice shattered the stillness, it roused her as if from a trance.

"Who's the thief, Dallas? Me or you?"

Squaring her shoulders, Troy went to see if Tom Elliot's punch had as much of a kick as he'd promised.

It was better than kicking herself for being a fool....

FOUR

WHEN TROY DRAGGED herself out of bed at seven the next morning, she vowed between gritted teeth to get even with Tom Elliot before either of them was much older. Her head was going to fall off, she knew it was going to fall off, and there was not a damn thing she could do about it. She staggered into her bathroom with one hand clutching the throbbing weight and the other groping blindly.

Steaming hot water pummeling her in the shower helped, and the aspirin she swallowed promised relief, even though it dissolved sadistically on her sensitive tongue. By the time she'd managed to dress in jeans and a gold cowl-neck sweater and brush her hair gingerly, she felt almost human.

Standing before the steam-clouded vanity mirror in her bathroom, Troy cleared the glass enough to see her reflection and camouflage her reddened eyes with makeup, trying to think dispassionately about the events of last night. In the inebriated hours before dawn, her best tactic had seemed to be a fast charge through forward enemy positions. She had definitely arrived at that decision at some point, although she couldn't remember exactly when or exactly what it had meant at the time.

But Troy realized that she would just have to play it by ear. She frowned at the reflection of a woman who appeared paler than usual, remembering the sense of loss Dallas had left her with.

It all seemed unreal now, those abandoned and confusing emotions he had ignited within her. But she knew that it had been real, because even as she thought about it, her body ached emptily. She leaned her weight on the hands braced on the vanity and stared at her reflection.

"Have an affair with him," she told herself

fiercely. "Take what you can get before the novelty wears off and he gets bored with you. You're twenty-eight years old; Lord knows, you're entitled to a fling if that's what you want."

But was it what she wanted? Did she really want to break a long-held rule and follow in the footsteps of so many of her friends—living for the moment rather than the future? Did she want to allow this man into her life and into her heart, knowing full well that she would suffer for it?

Because, dammit, she was already half in love with him....

That was what had shocked her last night in the arms of a man she barely knew—not morals or scruples, but the sudden and certain knowledge of what she was beginning to feel for him.

"He thinks you've had a dozen lovers," she told her reflection with faint bitterness, "and it doesn't matter to him. That should tell you something, idiot. He may be obsessed with you, but it's a lead pipe cinch he won't take you home to meet his mother!"

With uncharacteristic violence Troy shoved the painful revelation away. He wanted to know her? Fine. She'd show him Troy Bennett wearing all her hats, and if his obsession survived the onslaught, she'd think of some other way to get him out of her life. She wouldn't let Dallas Cameron hurt her.

Bryce had done his usual perfect job in clearing up after the party; the only evidence of the night before were the flowers, sent to the hostess this morning, that were now decorating the entrance hall and sitting room. On her way through to the dining room Troy checked several of the cards accompanying the arrangements.

"The hospital as usual, Miss Troy?"

She looked over her shoulder as she paused in the doorway to the formal dining room, no longer able to be surprised by the butler's soundless approach. "Send them around later this morning, Bryce," she said, glancing back at the colorful flowers. "The geriatrics wing, I think."

"Yes, miss; I'll take care of it."

"Of course, you will," Troy murmured, stepping into the dining room.

Jamie was seated halfway down the long table, a newspaper spread out before him and a cleared plate pushed to one side. He looked up as she entered, his blue eyes bright and appraising. "Morning, *mon enfant*."

"Morning." Troy went immediately to the antique sideboard, and poured out a cup of steaming black coffee.

"The punch?" Jamie questioned sympathetically.

Troy threw him a grimace as she sat down across from him at the table. "It's not supposed to be so obvious; the cosmetics companies claim that they can hide anything."

"Try those eyedrops that 'get the red out' instead," Jamie suggested, deadpan.

"Breakfast, Miss Troy?" Bryce asked from behind her.

"No, thank you. Just the coffee."

"She'll have toast and fruit," Jamie instructed.

Bryce left the room, and Troy stared across at her very large and very dear friend with a faint smile. "Jamie—"

"You have to eat."

"And you're mother-henning me again, friend."

"Somebody has to."

Troy sat back in her chair and sighed softly.

"Maybe you're right; I can't seem to take care of myself these days."

Jamie looked at her steadily for a moment, then calmly folded his paper and set it aside. "Not entirely the punch," he said slowly. "Something else is bothering you, *chérie*?"

She didn't answer until Bryce, after silently placing fruit and toast in front of her, had left the room again. Ignoring the fruit, she picked up a piece of toast and nibbled absently. "Someone," she replied finally.

"Cameron," Jamie guessed in the tone of a man who knew it was more than a guess. "I saw him last night."

Troy summoned a smile. "Before or after you disappeared into Daddy's den with your cronies for the game?"

"Before. He was talking to the general, and I had to wait to gather the last of my 'cronies.' "

She nodded, knowing that the general had spent the larger part of the evening—along with several other men—in the den with Jamie, playing poker. "Did the general win as usual?" she asked idly, finishing the toast more to placate Jamie than out of hunger.

"As usual, and stop changing the subject. Is Cameron going to be a problem?"

"Going to be?" Troy smiled in spite of herself. "He already *is* a problem. But he's my problem, Jamie."

"You're going to see him again?" Jamie asked carefully.

Before Troy could answer, Bryce stepped opportunely into the room. "Mr. Cameron to see you, Miss Troy."

"Send him in." Troy shrugged rather helplessly at Jamie's startled look. With the first real amusement of the morning she wondered what the two men were going to make of each other.

Dallas strode into the room a moment later wearing a blue turtleneck sweater over dark slacks, his black hair a little windblown, and Troy felt her heart skip a beat. Oh, *damn*, how was she going to be able to keep things from getting serious when just the sight of him affected her like this?

"Good morning—" Dallas began cheerfully, breaking off abruptly as he saw Jamie rising from his chair.

"Dallas Cameron," Troy murmured, "James

Riley." Deliberately she didn't add any explanatory information. The two men shook hands, eyeing each other, she thought wryly, like stray cats preparing to be either amiable or hostile, depending upon how things went.

Deciding to avoid the issue, she asked Dallas briskly, "Have you had breakfast?"

He nodded slowly, still eyeing Jamie thoughtfully. "Yes, thanks."

"Fine. Then we'll be on our way." She rose from her chair.

Jamie resumed his own chair, donning the inscrutable expression he wore whenever his *"enfant"* was about to get herself into trouble. He addressed himself to Troy in his deep, lazy voice. "Making the rounds today as usual?"

Troy realized what he was asking. "Uh-huh. Mr. Cameron is . . . tagging along for the day."

Jamie's penetrating light blue eyes shifted to Dallas. "Mmm. Well, he looks to be in good shape. Might even be able to keep up with you."

Biting back a laugh at Dallas's rather stiff expression. Troy hastily made her way from the room. "See you later, Jamie," she called over her shoulder.

"Take care, *mon enfant*," Jamie called back meaningfully.

Troy snared her sheepskin jacket from Bryce's hands before he could offer to help her into it, and had the front door open before the butler could perform the task. Clearly aggrieved, Bryce did manage to halt her characteristic rush with a message.

"Mr. Elliot just phoned, Miss Troy. He asked me to remind you of the rehearsal this afternoon."

"Lord, is he up already?" Troy murmured, more to herself than anyone else. She shrugged into her jacket, highly conscious of Dallas standing just behind her. "The man's stomach must be cast iron, and I hate to think of what his head is made of. If he calls again, Bryce, tell him I'll be there."

"Of course, Miss Troy."

She breezed out the door and down the steps to the front drive, with Dallas right behind her.

Parked in the drive with the engine already running was a low-slung, audibly powerful Porsche. It was strikingly, gleamingly black, top down, and promising hell with the lid off.

Troy paused a moment to watch Dallas's face

assume a somewhat guarded expression as he saw the car, and she challenged coolly, "D'you mind being driven by a woman?"

"Not at all," he answered immediately. "In fact, I'd consider it an honor."

"Then get in." She climbed in the driver's side and waited while Dallas, who'd politely closed the door for her, went around to the passenger side and carefully folded his tall length into the cramped quarters.

His door shut firmly, Dallas looked across at Troy with lifted brows. "Where are we off to?" he asked cheerfully.

She put the car into gear and sent him a wicked smile. "First, we're going to pick up a monkey. You get to hold him."

"Great," Dallas murmured rather faintly, his fingers digging reflexively into the dashboard as the little car erupted from the driveway and into the quiet street with a roar.

It didn't take ten minutes for Dallas to find out that Troy was the wildest driver this side of the Indy 500. Not unsafe—just wild. And in a city filled with innumerable cops, they weren't stopped once. She waved cheerfully at uniformed officers she encountered, and all of them waved back, their faces set in the identical expression of resignation.

By the time they reached the pet shop that was obviously their destination, Dallas had managed to get a grip on himself. He did *not* like being driven—by anyone, man or woman. It was, he'd long ago decided, a dislike of surrendering control to someone else. He'd even accepted that dislike to the point of learning to fly the company jet himself rather than sit back and let the company pilot earn his pay.

And he had a sneaking suspicion that Troy knew, or had guessed, his particular phobia. The little witch...

As the car stopped in front of the pet shop he forced his hands to assume a relaxed pose on the dashboard. "Where," he asked carefully, "did you learn to drive?"

"Learn?" Her smile was gentle. "Why, it came naturally. D'you want to wait here while I go get the monkey?"

Dallas nodded. He didn't trust himself to speak. Watching as she disappeared into the shop, he reviewed the list of questions branded into his brain since he'd walked into her house only a few minutes before.

Who was James Riley? What "rehearsal" had Elliot called to remind Troy of? Why was she getting a monkey? How was it that all the cops in D.C. seemed to know her to the point of being clearly resigned to her wild driving?

After a moment Dallas wryly elected to keep his questions to himself. He'd already seen the results of provoking her; it was not something he cared to see happen again. Besides, he fully expected this day with her to answer some, if not all, of the questions. Those that went unanswered, he decided, he could deal with.

Maybe.

The monkey, complete with red jacket and hat, was named Jinks, and busied himself by combing through Dallas's hair during the blessedly brief trip to their next destination, an orphanage.

The privately sponsored institution was overflowing with children, all of whom welcomed Troy with a joyous enthusiasm only slightly surpassed by their welcome of Jinks. Dallas, watching in fascination from the sidelines, noted Troy's obvious affection for the kids, and marveled at her endless patience with them. Odd, he thought, remembering the short fuse to her temper that he'd encountered once or twice.

They spent two hours at the orphanage and Dallas, instinctively comfortable with children, found himself answering their questions and drawn into their games. Too constantly aware of Troy to become completely absorbed, he nonetheless enjoyed the contact with the young and lively minds.

From the orphanage, where Jinks stayed behind with the kids, the little black Porsche weaved erratically through increasingly busy streets, stopping briefly at a fast-food restaurant where Troy solemnly treated him to a burger and fries. She chatted amiably to him during the meal, quite obviously making small talk and clearly aware that he realized that. And her striking green-gold/gold-green eyes coolly invited him to have another shot at provoking her temper by resisting her clear determination to keep things casual.

Dallas responded with easy cheerfulness.

The stops following their short lunch were

made in such quick succession that he was left more than a little bemused. At each halt Troy introduced him casually as "Cameron—my sparring partner." She never explained the somewhat cryptic introduction, and, although Dallas garnered more than a few curious looks, he began to realize that no one who knew Troy was very much surprised by anything she said or did.

Later the Porsche visited three private homes, where Troy briskly discussed security systems with three clearly fascinated and very wealthy men, then made the rounds of several businesses where systems had already been installed. Dallas quickly discovered that Troy was highly respected in her profession, her advice immediately accepted as the word of an expert.

Carefully and silently gathering information from words dropped here and there and from what he saw, Dallas began adding pieces to the puzzle of Troy Bennett.

Like a chameleon she blended in perfectly with her surroundings—whatever they might be. She discussed electronics with and swore fluently and amiably at electricians, spoke patiently to children without talking down to them, dealt confidently with businessmen on an equal footing. She hurled the Porsche around town as if it were a guided missile.

There were several references made as to the whereabouts of Jamie and more than one mention of an upcoming charity event in which Troy was apparently to participate. There was also a clue that Troy's business was called TB Security and was run out of her home.

Between stops Dallas clutched the dashboard and tried to keep his eyes off the dizzily passing scenery. "TB Security?" he asked once, wondering if it stood for her name and nothing else.

Troy threw him a bland look that made him acutely uneasy, especially since it took her eyes off the road, and explained politely. "Teddy Bear."

"Teddy Bear," he repeated faintly.

"Uh-huh. A security blanket—like that."

"Oh."

"I wanted to call it B and E Security, or Nickel to Dime Security. You know, B and E for breaking and entering, and Nickel to Dime for the time one generally gets for breaking and entering. Five to ten years."

"Oh, Lord," Dallas said.

"Mmm. That's what Jamie said. So I decided not."

Dallas made a sudden decision and knowingly took his life in his hands—or rather in hers, he thought—by chancing one probing question. "You can tell me it's none of my business, but—who's Jamie?"

"James Riley."

Dallas silently counted to ten. "I know. But *who* is he?"

She didn't look at him. "A very dear friend."

"I see."

"I doubt it," Troy murmured as she hurled the Porsche around a turn.

Deciding to leave the potentially explosive subject alone, Dallas mentally added up his list of things they had in common. He meant to prove to Troy that they had a solid basis aside from chemistry on which to build a lasting relationship.

Although now considered a businessman, Dallas had founded his own company on expertise in electronics; they had that in common. A casual word from one of her clients had told him that she was a licensed pilot; they had that in common. The Porsche told him they both favored small, powerful sports cars. They both knew, understood, and loved art. They both liked children.

It was a good list. Couples had passed their silver wedding anniversaries having less than that in common, Dallas thought.

But...

He had called her a thief, and that one word was standing between them. He didn't believe that she *was* a thief—if he ever had in the beginning. But he had called her a thief, and that could never be taken back. Of course, he could tell her that he didn't think that now. But she wouldn't believe him.

How to convince her...?

The last stop of the afternoon was at an auditorium, where Tom Elliot was waiting with his band.

Dallas was a sensible man. Usually. The green-eyed monster didn't trouble him. Usually. And he was well aware of the hazards of holding a stick of dynamite in one hand and a lighted match in the other.

Usually.

"Is he another *friend*?" Dallas muttered as they

walked down the dim aisle toward the lighted stage and the noisy confusion there.

Troy stopped. She turned slowly and looked up at him. "He is."

Unable to read her changing eyes and changing mood, and unable to stop the words and emotions rising in him, Dallas pressed on. "And is he the reason you were hung over this morning?"

She crossed her arms over her breasts. "No. He was the instrument, I suppose you could say. Not the reason." Her voice was very even.

"Maybe I shouldn't have said good night so early," Dallas said tightly.

"When I want a watchdog, I'll buy a Doberman."

"Troy—"

"You're pushing, Cameron. And it stops right here. Or everything stops . . . right here."

His eyes adjusting to the dimness, Dallas looked down into her glittering green ones. *She'll never be able to hide her anger from me*, he thought, and didn't know if that would turn out to be good or bad. He looked toward the stage, where the blond, handsome, very famous and charming man was cheerfully ribbing his pianist. Then he looked back down at Troy.

"I've never been jealous before," he said quietly.

Troy felt her heart jump suddenly. Oh, *damn* the man! Why hadn't he done what nine out of ten men would have done—exploded? Why did he have to admit jealousy openly in a quiet and rueful tone that left her without the weapon of anger?

She hadn't meant to explain anything, but Troy was not surprised to hear her voice saying flatly, "If I'd wanted to get involved with Tommy, I would have done so years ago. He's a friend. I have lots of friends."

Dallas looked down at her for a long, silent moment. Then his hands lifted to rest on her shoulders, lightly, tentatively, as though he half expected her to shrug the touch away. "Troy..." He shook his head slightly. "It wouldn't bother me so much if you'd just meet me halfway."

"I don't know what you're talking about."

"Yes, you do." His hands tightened. "There's been a challenge in your eyes since I first walked into your house this morning. You've dropped bits of information and worn them like chips on your shoulder, expecting—hoping—that I'd provoke you and give you a reason to...to call off our agreement. You've drawn a line between us, and you're daring me to step over it."

"If you don't like the game—" she began hotly.

He gave her one quick shake. "It isn't a game! That's what I'm trying to make you understand. *It isn't a game*. You're not winning points for being stubborn, and I'm not winning them for being patient. I want to be a part of your life, Troy, and I want you to be a part of mine."

Troy stared up at him, mentally resisting, physically stiff.

Dallas returned her stare, feeling frustration well up inside of him. "What are you afraid of?" he demanded softly. "Me?"

She stepped back, shrugging away his hands. In a voice so low, he barely caught the words, she murmured, "No. Me." Then she went down the aisle and climbed the steps to the brightly lit stage.

He followed more slowly, stopping short of the stage to take a seat in the second row. All things considered, he decided that he really didn't want to have to shake hands with Tom Elliot. And he needed the dim privacy of the seats; he needed to think.

"Hi, Blondie," Tom called cheerfully as Troy tossed her jacket to the grinning drummer and approached the piano.

"Hi," she returned calmly, picking up a tall stool on the way and hefting it like a weapon. "Any last requests before I kill you?"

"The punch?"

"In spades. I woke up with somebody else's head this morning."

Tom lifted his shoulders in a shrug and spread his hands defenselessly. "I told you it had a kick," he reminded innocently.

"Uh-huh." Troy sighed as she set the stool beside the piano and climbed up on it. "I am definitely going to kill you. Once for that damn punch, and once for roping me into what's going to go down in history as this infamous duet."

"I'd like to rope you into joining the band permanently."

"Forget it, chum."

It was Tom's turn to sigh. "Don't you think I get tired of hearing the sound of my own voice?" he asked in a long-suffering tone. "I swear if one more hostess archly asks me to sing for my supper, I'll—"

Amused, Troy said, "It's your own fault for living in a city full of parties and hostesses. Live in Hollywood instead; there are so many entertainers out there, they'd never notice you."

Tom grimaced slightly. "Not a chance."

"Not going to accept the studio's offer, then?"

"Oh, no. I've seen what happens when some misguided studio decides to turn a singer into an actor; I can deal with the potshots from music critics, but I don't need film critics blasting me as well."

Smiling at him, Troy picked up a sheaf of music from the top of the piano. "Probably a wise decision, although you'd make a terrific actor."

"Why, thank—"

"You're pure ham."

"—you very much!" Tom's pleased tone turned indignant on the last three words.

"You're welcome."

Tom leaned an elbow on the piano. "While we're attacking personalities, was that Ace Cameron I saw you come in with?"

"Whose personality are you attacking with that question?" Troy inquired dryly.

"Don't avoid the question."

"It's him."

"Mmm. Should I ask why you brought him along?"

"I'd appreciate it if you wouldn't."

"In other words, mind my own business?"

"Those words cover it nicely."

"I only wondered," Tom said innocently, "because it looked as if you two were having a disagreement up there in the aisle."

"You see too much, Tommy."

"Shut up and sing, huh?"

"Exactly."

"Oh, all right. But if you need a shoulder, Blondie—"

"I'll keep you in mind."

For the next two hours, Dallas sat quietly, watching and listening as Troy rehearsed several songs with Tom Elliot and his band. Her voice, though untrained, was richly powerful and huskily seductive, and Dallas wondered idly if anyone had ever told her just how good she was.

A chameleon, that's what she was. As changeable and unpredictable as a spring storm.

And afraid of . . . herself.

Since he wasn't a vain man, Dallas didn't believe that by that admission she meant she was afraid of how he could make her feel. Troy was a blunt woman; if she'd meant, *I'm afraid of how you make me feel*, then that's what she would have said. No, for some reason he didn't—yet— understand, she was afraid of herself.

He turned that over in his mind, examined it from every angle, held it up to the mental searchlight that had always penetrated to truth. But there was still darkness, because he didn't yet know enough about Troy to be able to see what was there.

And then there was the matter of how to convince her that he didn't consider her a thief. Dallas Cameron, boardroom strategist, tireless planner, went to work on that problem.

With an effort that left her head aching, Troy put Dallas from her mind long enough to rehearse with Tom. But during the brief intermissions between songs, while Tom discussed various changes with the band, echoes of their conversation—confrontation?—disturbed her.

"You're not winning points for being stubborn, and I'm not winning them for being patient."

"I want to be a part of your life...."

"It isn't a game!"

She didn't look out into the dim auditorium. She wouldn't let herself look to see if he was still out there watching. But reluctantly she realized that his accusation had been deserved. She *had* been wearing a chip on her shoulder all day. She had behaved with a grim determination, and that bothered her suddenly.

What was wrong with her? If she didn't want the man in her life, she had only to tell him that in no uncertain terms; he wasn't, she knew intuitively, the kind of man to press his—attentions?—on a woman who really didn't want him around.

Why all the hedging? she wondered broodingly. Hedging and halfhearted protests—and "agreements," for God's sake. Why couldn't she just flatly tell the man that she wasn't interested?

"Blondie! Hey, kid, pay attention!"

Snapping back to her surroundings, Troy bent

her mind to the songs, and tried to ignore Tom's curious, speculative look. "Let's see. Where were we?"

"I don't know where *you* were, but—"

"Sing, Tommy."

"Uh . . . right."

After the rehearsal was finally concluded to their satisfaction, Tom cheerfully released the band and then reminded Troy politely that her *escort* was still waiting for her. With a faint grimace she waved and collected her jacket, going down the steps and into the still-dim auditorium. A patch of darkness detached itself from the second row and moved out into the aisle to join her.

"You two sing well together," Dallas said as they started for the lobby.

"Thanks. Tommy has a wonderful voice."

"So have you."

Stiffly Troy replied, "I wasn't fishing."

"I didn't think you were."

Troy said nothing more. She was half puzzled and half wary; the even, controlled tone of his voice bothered her. Darkness had fallen while they'd been inside, and they walked beneath the harsh glare of the parking-lot lights in silence. Silently they got into the Porsche. Silently they made the drive back to Troy's house.

It was Dallas who broke the strained and uncomfortable silence when they reached her house. Ignoring the silver-gray Mercedes—obviously his, she realized for the first time—parked in her drive, Dallas joined her on the walkway, and said evenly, "Mind if I come in for a few minutes?"

She wanted to say that she did, indeed, mind. Wanted to—but couldn't somehow. Without speaking, she led the way up the walk and into the house.

Bryce, for once a second ahead of her, opened the door for them. The butler took her jacket with a faintly gratified expression, telling her in his curiously paternal yet formal tone that dinner would be ready in an hour.

Troy hesitated for a moment, then looked up at Dallas. "Join me?"

"Maybe we'd better talk first," he replied flatly.

The rebuff stung, but it roused no anger in Troy. He was entitled, she thought, to that shot. She led the way into an informal den off the main hall and went immediately to a built-in bar in one corner, glancing back over her shoulder. "Drink?"

"Dutch courage?" he asked.

It didn't sound like a taunt.

"D'you want a drink?" she repeated quietly.

"Whiskey."

She fixed the drinks silently, carrying his across to him and then sitting down in one corner of an overstuffed love seat (and why had she chosen that? she wondered) with her own glass of wine. Sipping the cool liquid, she watched him prowl, catlike, around the room.

While the silence lengthened he gazed at the paintings on the walls, the comfortable over-stuffed furniture, the collection of figurines from *Alice's Adventures in Wonderland* in a curio cabinet. Almost without thinking, he realized that this was Troy's room. He didn't know how he knew.

Abruptly he said, "It's amazing how reasonable you become when I get angry."

As he turned suddenly to face her Troy found something very interesting to look at in her wine-glass. "It isn't that," she said almost inaudibly, wondering just what in hell it *was*.

"Oh, did I touch a nerve with something I said earlier?" he asked sardonically.

She said nothing.

Dallas began prowling again, though his eyes rarely left her. "Well, just on the off chance that I *did* touch a nerve, why don't I enlarge on the theme?"

Troy opened her mouth to speak, then closed it. Because he was entitled to this, too, she realized dimly.

"We'll start with your *stated* determination to keep me out of your life," Dallas began calmly, still pacing the room. "You told me that you didn't want to get involved with me. But you invited me to your party. Then you told me a second time that you wouldn't get involved with me. But you agreed to allow me to...get to know you. Knowing—*knowing*—that this spark between us is very nearly too damn hot to handle. Didn't you?" he pounced suddenly.

Troy almost jumped. "Yes," she agreed softly, still gazing fixedly at her glass.

"Fine." His voice was hard, controlled. "On to your challenging attitude today. All day long you've been daring me to step over that neat little line you've drawn between us. You've tried your best to provoke *me* into provoking you. Oh, not openly. Just little things—a word here and there, a look. Well, Miss Bennett, did I get any points for being patient? Did I?"

His second pounce didn't catch Troy by surprise. She lifted her gaze finally, her eyes unerringly locating him where he stood by the fireplace. She looked at him, still not speaking.

Dallas laughed shortly. "You're good with games, lady. And we've both learned how to play them, haven't we? I learned in the boardroom; I don't know where you learned. All the nice little civilized games meant to avoid honesty at all costs. 'Don't be honest,' it says in the rule book. 'Don't let anyone else know what you're thinking or feeling, or you'll lose.' In the boardroom I might lose a lucrative deal; what would you lose, Troy?"

She wanted to reply, *"Myself."* but she didn't know why. She said nothing. Her gaze dropped back to the safety of the wineglass.

"Cat got your tongue?" he asked with mocking lightness. Then he laughed again before she could respond. "One of your nicknames, isn't it? But I gather it's spelled with a *K*. Such a...revealing nickname."

Troy knew now why he was sometimes called Genghis Khan. He was a master of verbal fencing. The scary thing was that the man was fighting fair; there was nothing cruel in his words, no strike below the belt. Just brutal honesty.

Suddenly, violently, Dallas said, "What's it going to take to convince you that this is not a game to me?"

She looked up again, and her eyes were wetly shimmering gold. "I knew," she said simply.

The violence draining away, Dallas moved slowly toward her, gazing into her fascinating eyes, riveted by something he saw deep within their golden pools.

"Games." Troy shook her head in an odd, rueful movement. "Did you ever notice that no one ever really loses in games? You beat me at chess; I beat you at tennis. You own Boardwalk: I own Park Place. It all evens out in the end. I concede gracefully, retire from the field. Or you do. Pride bruised, but ego essentially intact.

"Where did I learn the games?" She watched as he came to sit on the loveseat, half turned toward her just as she was half turned toward him. "I'm a Rhodes Scholar," she said suddenly. "Studied at the Sorbonne. But I was too young," she added, brooding.

Dallas waited silently for a moment, then asked softly, "Where did you learn the games?"

"Everywhere." She laughed without making a sound. "Europe. The Orient. Here. I learned at the Court of Saint James. In embassies all over the world. From watching and listening to the—master gamesmen."

"Your father was a diplomat?" Dallas probed carefully.

She nodded almost absently, but then her mood changed swiftly. "Games," she said tightly. "Nice, safe games. I learned how to play before I knew *why*. And then when I knew why, it seemed wiser to play by the rules."

"So you decided to play by the rules with me?"

Troy again laughed soundlessly. "That's the ironic thing. You've already pointed out that I've been . . . unreasonable. I guess the psychiatrists would say that I've been 'giving out conflicting signals.' Saying one thing, doing something else. Pretending it was a game when I knew it wasn't."

FIVE

Troy smiled at him, a tiny, rueful smile that tugged at his heart. "Like you said—if you don't play the game, you could lose. If I pretended it was a game, I couldn't lose . . . anything important."

Dallas fought his impulse to touch her, determined to do nothing to disturb this new and fragile harmony. "I believe I told you once," he said seriously, "that I'd never hurt you."

She shook her head slightly. "It's not the same thing. I'm not afraid of being hurt, Dallas; life is full of hurts. I'm afraid of losing a part of myself."

"To me?"

"To you. Because of you. I don't know that it would happen. But I knew—even though I wouldn't admit it—that you weren't playing games. And that scared the hell out of me."

"And so—the conflicting signals?"

Troy nodded. She looked down, turned the wineglass in her hand, and studied the reflection of light off the liquid. "And now I don't know what to do," she confessed softly.

"Be honest with me."

Basically honest in spite of the games, Troy thought about what it would mean to be honest with Dallas. And she knew. Vulnerability, a terrifying vulnerability. *You knew,* she told herself scornfully. *You knew what you were doing when you opened the door to let him into your life. You knew. And you know what you've already lost to him.*

"Troy?" He reached out tentatively to touch her shoulder, his arm lying along the back of the love seat. "I meant what I said before; I only want to get to know you. No games, no chip on your shoulder." He hesitated for a moment, then added, "I want very badly to be your lover, but I won't press you on that."

She looked at him with clear, rueful eyes. "Won't you?"

Dallas grinned a little. "Well . . . no more than I can help."

After a silent moment Troy reached over to press a small button on the end table beside the love seat. When Bryce came soundlessly into the room a minute later, she waited for Dallas's slight nod, then told the butler, "Mr. Cameron will be joining me for dinner, Bryce."

It was a peculiar evening, Troy decided later. They were both a bit wary; having agreed to honesty, each was mindful that it wouldn't be easy.

Dallas had shrewdly hit on a major stumbling block between them; the games they both played so well. Oh, in the right situation, both of them would be considered brutally honest. But there was honesty, and then there was *honesty*. He was an honest man and she was an honest woman— and both played the games because that was the way it was done.

And although neither spoke the doubt aloud, both were conscious of the uncertainty of dispensing with games and rules—and fumbling their way.

They talked over dinner—guardedly, cautiously. Strictly casual, because there was, after all, a limit to the emotion it was wise to provoke in a single evening. Dallas did ask where Jamie was and, although he looked at her rather sharply when she briefly replied that Jamie was "busy," he said nothing more about it.

Dallas left late that evening, asking quietly if he might "tag along" with her the next day. Never one to look back in regret after finally having come to terms with herself, Troy agreed.

She said good night to Bryce and climbed the stairs thoughtfully, mentally going over the events of the day and wondering what she had foolishly let herself in for. She met Jamie on the landing as he was coming down from the third floor, which contained their work area.

"It's set up," Jamie told her.

Troy looked at him absently, his words sinking in only marginally. "Is it? Good. That's good. We'll go over everything tomorrow night, okay? Good night, Jamie."

"*Mon enfant?*" He caught one of her hands in a huge paw. "Are you all right?"

"Do you remember once telling me," she murmured, "that if I ever met a man who could keep up with me, he and I would both be in trouble?"

"I remember."

She sighed. "I think—I very much think, my friend—that I've met him. My Waterloo."

Jamie squeezed her hand gently. "It's about time."

Troy laughed in spite of herself. "You're a lot of help! Are you going to sound the cannons while I go down in defeat?"

He grinned, his broad, stolid face wearing the expression with a curiously endearing unfamiliarity. "No, but I'll be watching the battle from the sidelines. It ought to be interesting, *chérie.*"

"You're on his side, damn you," she told him ruefully.

"No. On yours. I just happen to believe that the two of you are on the same side."

Troy yawned suddenly. "That's too cryptic for me. I'll see you in the morning, Jamie."

"Good night, *mon enfant.*" He watched her

head toward her bedroom, then shook his head slightly and headed for his own.

Characteristically always willing and able to live with her own decisions, Troy startled Dallas the next day by seemingly becoming a different woman. The chip on her shoulder was gone as though it had never existed; the cool challenge in her incredible eyes vanished.

Bemused, intrigued, and half wary that she was just in an unusual mood that would pass, Dallas nonetheless took advantage of it.

Their day was more or less a repeat of the day before. They visited a different orphanage, different clients. Troy took the children a basketful of kittens, and Dallas saw her unobtrusively slip a check to one of the administrators while she was talking to her. He said nothing about it.

The clients were dealt with briskly, questions answered and problems handled smoothly. Losing her temper only once, and that with an electrician who'd promised repairs and failed to deliver, she swore like a sailor as she talked to him over the phone and never once looked or sounded anything but a lady.

And that, Dallas realized suddenly, was the key

to Troy Bennett. She was a *lady*. A misused word these days, he knew, but it fit her perfectly. She was both sexy and tough; the beautiful, smooth exterior sheathing tempered steel beneath. Her soft, clear voice was capable of both deep gentleness and icy command. There was a curious pioneer strength reflected in her remarkable eyes, the kind of strength that could cradle a baby on one hip and a rifle on the other—and knew how to handle both.

Absorbing that, Dallas probed cautiously into her past during the moments they spent alone while she hurled the Porsche around town. She answered his questions readily but briefly, letting him know that she really didn't like to talk about herself. But at least she answered.

"So your father was a diplomat?"

"Uh-huh."

"You've obviously seen a lot of the world."

"Most of it, I sometimes think."

"And your mother?"

Troy didn't have to ask him to clarify the question. "She was an actress when Dad met her. French. She was also a very talented artist, and that talent won out in the end."

"Which explains your knowledge of art."

"I grew up with it."

"I see."

Suddenly, unemotionally, Troy said, "They were killed years ago. Terrorists."

Dallas looked at her swiftly. "I'm sorry, Troy."

A nod acknowledged his sympathy. Determined not to talk anymore about that painful part of her life, she changed the subject. "You've been curious about Jamie, I know. He was my guardian for a couple of years before I came of age. Dad trusted him more than any man he'd ever known; they were very good friends for years. He's my godfather."

Studying her with his full attention since he'd grown accustomed to Troy's habit of turning the Porsche on a dime, Dallas noted curiously, "Am I wrong in thinking he uses French endearments with you? His name's Irish."

"So's he." Troy smiled a little and said calmly, "He spent a lot of time in France, and always loved the language. That's where he met my mother and fell in love with her."

Dallas thought about that for a moment. "He

was in love with your mother, and yet he and your father were good friends?"

"Very good friends." She laughed softly. "It wasn't a case of a romantic triangle. Jamie's love for my mother was a very special thing."

Dallas reflected silently that it must, indeed, have been special.

"And since you obviously didn't recognize his name," she murmured, "I should tell you that Jamie is also one of the most famous stunt pilots in aviation history."

"Good Lord. The name rang a bell, but I just couldn't place it. I suppose he taught you to fly?"

Troy frowned for a moment, obviously puzzled. Then her frown cleared. "You've been paying attention, I see. Mr. Styles mentioned my being a pilot yesterday."

"Yes." Dallas smiled slightly. "I never did hire that detective, Troy. I'm finding out about you without hired help."

Another frown flitted across her brow, brief but troubled.

"Does that bother you?" he asked perceptively.

"I don't know. Maybe." She seemed to shake the thought away. "Tell me about yourself."

Dallas wondered if he should stick with the point, but decided not to. "There's not a lot to tell."

"He said modestly," she murmured.

Making a grab for the dashboard as the Porsche swung merrily around a corner, Dallas said suddenly, "I *don't* like to be driven."

She started laughing. "I suspected as much!"

"Witch."

"Flatterer." Troy sent him an amused glance, and immediately slowed the little car's headlong rush. "I wondered how long it'd take you to—"

"Swallow my pride?" Dallas supplied dryly.

"Something like that. Anyway, I promise to have a little more regard for my passenger's nerves from now on."

"I'd appreciate that."

"So. Tell me about yourself."

Dallas looked at her for a moment, then began to speak in a deliberate litany. "I'm thirty-six years old. I was born and raised in California. I have a younger brother and sister, two nieces and one nephew, and my parents live in California. I graduated from M.I.T. with a degree in electronics. After graduation I borrowed every cent I could get my hands on to start my own company, and I've built from there."

"And very well too," she murmured.

"Thank you," he responded, then went on with the recital. "I have no vices that I'm aware of. I'm reasonably neat and can cook in a pinch. I possess something of a temper—as you're aware—but generally manage to fight fair even when I'm mad."

"As I'm also aware," Troy noted wryly.

"Mmm. I have a fondness for Italian food, adventure movies, mystery novels, sailing, hang gliding, children, animals, and redheaded cat burglars."

Troy silently rode out the roller-coaster surges of her heart at that last fond remark, trying to ignore it. "Hang gliding," she murmured. "You're more reckless than you seem."

"I'm also," he added deliberately, "adept at mountain climbing, and I hold a sharpshooter classification with most handguns."

"Now where did you pick that up?" she wondered curiously.

"My father's career Army. And a great teacher."

"I see." Troy mulled over the information.

Clearly, she realized, Dallas was a man of action. Hang gliding *alone* required strong nerves and cool self-command. And he was also adept at sailing and mountain climbing—hardly a sedentary life-style in spite of his white-collar occupation.

Troy pulled the Porsche into a parking space in front of a museum where her company provided electronic security, and took a moment to study Dallas thoughtfully. "It seems there's more to you than I'd realized, Mr. Cameron," she observed.

"I'm glad you realize it now," he responded.

Dallas tagged along with Troy for several days, their relationship remaining on its cautiously amiable footing. They shared casual lunches during the day and peaceful dinners each night at Troy's house, and they learned more about each other.

The subject of Troy's nocturnal activities having been tacitly avoided by both, it wasn't until Friday night that the issue was finally confronted. An unavoidable business appointment had caused Dallas to cut short their day together, and on impulse he stopped by her house around nine that night.

Bryce opened the door to him, and Dallas immediately noticed the butler's faintly guarded expression. Stepping inside the hall to avoid the possibility of having the door closed in his face, he asked casually, "Is she here?"

Bryce's butlerly composure didn't falter, but he hesitated for an infinite second. "If you would care to wait in the sitting room, sir?"

Absorbing Bryce's refusal to commit himself, Dallas merely nodded slightly and went to wait. He had been in the sitting room for only five minutes when the butler returned, and politely asked to be accompanied upstairs. Following Bryce up to the third floor, Dallas silently put two and two together and knew, with a faintly sinking sensation, that he had arrived at the correct conclusion when the butler opened a set of double doors into what was clearly a . . . command center.

The room was large and airy, and crammed to capacity with electronic equipment. There were three separate computer terminals, a wall-size bulletin board with cryptic diagrams tacked to it, and a huge oak desk covered with papers and an elaborate phone system. And in the center of the room, bending over diagrams on a large work table, were Troy and Jamie.

Troy straightened slowly as Bryce closed the doors behind Dallas, and she looked across at him gravely. Without glancing at her companion, she murmured, "Would you give us a few minutes, please, Jamie?"

The big man shot a glance at Dallas and then, silently, left through a connecting door leading into another room.

"Does that outfit mean what I think?" Dallas asked tautly, obviously referring to her black pants, sweater, and the black gloves and ski mask that were tucked into her belt.

Troy leaned a hip on the table's corner, continuing to meet his gaze levelly. "I have a job to do," she told him quietly. "Tonight."

"Let me go with you."

She shook her head, and Dallas took a quick step forward. "Troy, I can't let you—"

Holding up a hand to stop him, Troy said reasonably, "Where've you been for the past five years? We both know I've done this before, and that I can take care of myself. Dallas, I don't need a Galahad." Softly she added, "I don't *want* a Galahad."

Dallas took a deep breath and released it slowly. Why, he asked himself, couldn't she have been the helpless, clinging type? But he knew why.

Because she wasn't that type. And he wouldn't have fallen in love with her if she had been.

"What *do* you want?" he asked finally.

Troy left the table, coming to stand before him, just within arm's reach. "Someone who understands that I can't be less than I am."

He looked down at her, grimacing slightly. "Women's lib," he muttered.

She smiled. "I'm not a card-carrying member. But I won't be protected like a hothouse flower. I'd smother."

"And I can't wipe out two million years of evolution," Dallas complained wryly. "For good or bad, the instinct is to protect—" The one you love, he finished silently.

"There's two million years of intellect as well," Troy pointed out.

"Instinct is stronger," Dallas told her. "I want to understand, Troy, but—"

She turned suddenly and took a few steps away

from him, then wheeled around to face him. The wounded look he had seen only once before was in her eyes, her golden eyes, and it made his heart ache.

"Then maybe this will help you to understand." She took a deep breath. "I told you that my parents were killed by terrorists."

"Yes."

"I was eighteen." Her voice was abrupt, hard-edged with an obvious effort of control. "In college. Two different governments and various law-enforcement agencies promised that the murderers would pay. Promised—but didn't deliver on the promise."

"Empty promises," Dallas realized slowly, the explanation of her disillusionment with promises becoming clear to him.

"Empty promises. Oh, they were sympathetic; they made all the right noises. But the bottom line was that since the terrorist group couldn't be proved responsible, nothing could be done. That's when I decided to do something about it myself."

"What did you do?" Dallas asked slowly.

"Using every spare moment and with Jamie's help, I began what you might call a paper search for some kind of proof. It took five years. And during that time I made a lot of the contacts that I find so useful now. I traveled all over the world checking leads, gathering data from every source I could find. I retained a rather well-known attorney to keep me advised on the legality of the proof I obtained."

She hesitated, then added softly, "I saw parts of the world I'd choose to forget if I could. I—still have nightmares sometimes." She lifted her chin suddenly. "But I found the proof. The people responsible for my parents' deaths paid for what they did.

"And I discovered then that I could do something about injustice. Nothing major, nothing spectacular. I loved art, and I knew that private collectors and museums were being ripped off; I was good at security systems. And I loved the excitement of pitting my wits against the problem. So I became a cat burglar. Although you may not believe it, I don't profit by what I do. I have a private investigator's license, and I am what might be termed an honorary member of Interpol."

Troy took a deep breath and finished dryly,

"And I haven't explained that much of myself to anyone for years—if I ever did."

"Thank you," Dallas said seriously.

She looked at him perceptively. "But you still—object—to my working tonight, don't you?"

He hesitated, certain that the wrong words would be more than a mistake. "It isn't that I doubt your ability. It isn't that I think what you do is wrong—"

"You don't think it's wrong?" she inquired, suddenly suspicious.

"No, I don't think it's wrong." He saw that Troy didn't believe him, but went on anyway. "What I object to is the risk. The edge of danger is a slippery place, Troy. I don't want anything to happen to you."

"Nothing will happen to me," she said carelessly, going over to the table and taking a last quick look at the diagram lying there.

"Troy—"

"Dallas, I'm going." She gave him a very direct look.

"I can't change your mind?" His voice was even.

"No."

"All right, then." Without another word he turned on his heel and left the room.

Troy stood there for a long moment, staring blankly after him. Somehow she was disappointed that he'd given in so easily, and her own disappointment irritated her. "Idiot," she muttered to herself. "You know you don't want him to interfere—so what's the problem?"

Since the room was at the front of the house, she heard the roar of Dallas's Mercedes as it pulled out of the drive, and a frown crossed her brow. He was definitely, angry; from the sound of his car, he couldn't wait to put distance between the two of them.

She bit her bottom lip, her fingers toying with the gloves tucked into her belt. *I'm right,* she thought violently. *I'm right not to let him interfere!* Troy had been in control of her own life too long to willingly relinquish that control. And if she backed down on this point, if she let Dallas interfere with her work, it would be the first step toward giving up control.

Something else they had in common, she realized dully: Neither wanted someone else in control. That was why she had so quickly seen his dislike of being a passenger; she was the same way herself. And that was not a good trait for two people to have in common. Two strong personalities could coexist, but not if they shared the same powerful will. Not if one was a man and one a woman, both living in a world where traditional values still held. And not if those two strong-minded people wanted to spend their lives together.

Misery washed over her suddenly, causing her to lean numbly against the table. She had known from the beginning that it would happen, but was unprepared for the pain she felt then. Love didn't frighten her, not loving or being loved; what frightened and hurt her was the knowledge that she was in love and that her love was impossible.

"*Mon enfant?*"

Troy blinked and looked up at Jamie, her hand automatically reaching for the diagram on the table and rolling it into a neat cylinder. The mark of a professional, she thought vaguely, was that he or she never allowed personal pain to interfere with the job at hand.

She was a professional.

"I'm ready, Jamie. Let's go."

His big hand came out to rest on her shoulder, and concerned blue eyes probed hers. "Maybe we should postpone the job. The house is supposed to be empty through the weekend; we'll go tomorrow."

Troy shook her head and pulled a smile from somewhere. "No. Mr. Jordan sounded very anxious about his jade figurine, and I promised to get it back to him tomorrow afternoon. Besides, the only security out there tonight is electronic; the guard dogs are supposed to be brought in tomorrow." She frowned a little, trying to think clearly. "Sloppy arrangement," she observed.

Jamie hesitated, obviously troubled. "I haven't been able to trace the deed to that house, *chérie*; we still don't know who owns it."

With an impatient shrug Troy started for the door. "What does it matter, Jamie? You saw Roberts around the place yesterday and today: he's obviously the owner."

"We've rushed this job," Jamie protested, following her. "We should have taken the time we usually do to verify everything. We only have Jordan's word for it that Roberts stole the figurine."

Troy was at the stairs by the time Jamie caught up. Still impatient, she told him, "Jordan had a legitimate reason for not reporting the theft; since his inheritance of the collection is still tied up in the courts, he wouldn't want to rock the boat by losing a piece—especially through negligence. We saw his house, Jamie, and you know as well as I do that his security system has holes big enough for an elephant to slide through."

While still speaking. Troy wondered with an aching part of her mind if Dallas would ever want to see her again. Probably not. And even if he did, what would be the use of going on with something that would never—could never—work? God, she was tired. . . .

"I don't like it," Jamie insisted with unusual force. "There are too many unknowns in this job. Too many—"

"We'll argue about it on the way," Troy said absently.

Jamie muttered a comical mixture of Irish, French, and purely American oaths as he followed her from the house.

Dallas hurled the Mercedes around a turn and checked his watch for the tenth time, fragmented thoughts flashing through his mind as he searched for conscious understanding of what he'd already realized intuitively.

Troy. A woman who could not be leashed, but only coaxed to walk by his side. *Willingly* she could be led; unwillingly she would never follow. She would give as much as she was given, take only what was taken from her. And she demanded freedom as a basic need that had nothing to do with the modern cry of equality. Troy had to be free to choose her own way, accepting the risks and the responsibilities that accompanied her choice. She could never be less than she was.

It would take a strong man to be able to live with that. It would take a strong man to persuade this proud woman to share his life.

Checking his watch again, Dallas smiled grimly and hurled the straining car around another corner.

Over his protests Troy left Jamie to wait in the car as she approached what she knew was a beautiful Colonial mansion. The darkened house was visible only by moonlight; it was set back from the road, and the two acres of land were enclosed within high brick walls that provided reasonable security and privacy.

She went over the west wall easily with the aid of a large oak tree, and dropped inside with a muffled thump. Crouching there for a long moment, she studied the house's lifeless appearance, then straightened and made her way silently through the dark, peaceful yard.

Once at the house, it took only minutes to locate the fusebox and disconnect the security system. Troy frowned briefly behind her ski mask. Sloppy. In fact, she decided, the security for this place was lax to the point of stupidity. Brushing the thought away, she uncoiled the nylon line from her belt and expertly threw the grappling hook up to catch on a third-floor balcony on the east side of the house.

It would have been simpler, she knew, to pick a lock on one of the ground-floor doors, but Troy preferred this way. The practice never hurt, and besides, she'd found it quicker to walk through only a single unfamiliar room rather than an entire unfamiliar house.

She "walked" up the wall, her gloved hands gripping the nylon line easily, until she reached the second-floor window that was her goal. Locking the line, she hung there long enough to check for the possibility of a second, less obvious, electronic screen, then used a thin probe to open the window far enough for her fingers to slide beneath the sash.

Within seconds she was inside the house. She stood for a moment, listening and allowing her eyes to adjust, then unhooked her flashlight and turned it on. Keeping the light at waist height, she swept it quickly around the room. A brick fireplace, dark and cold, with a beautiful lithograph framed above the mantel. Built-in bookshelves on either side, filled with expensive leather-bound volumes. A thick, light carpet. In one corner a comfortably overstuffed wing chair and reading lamp. Several other chairs. A large, neatly bare walnut desk.

Troy focused her attention on the bookshelves behind the desk. Crossing the room, she gripped the flashlight between her teeth and carefully shifted books from one shelf onto the desk. If she had planned a safe for this room, she would have—

There! Behind the books was a sliding panel. She opened the panel and found the safe. A few moments work had the safe open, and Troy mentally reviewed the description of the figurine before reaching inside. In the narrow beam of light she identified an unwise amount of cash stacked neatly, a long black jeweler's case, a bound sheaf of negotiable bonds, and one chamois pouch about the size of her hand.

She removed the pouch, carefully untied the leather thong binding it, and examined the jade figurine exposed to her light. Bingo, Very old, very beautiful, and priceless.

Tucking the pouch securely in her tool belt, Troy quickly erased all evidence of her visit, closing the safe and placing the books back on their shelf. Then she headed for the window, unusually relieved to be virtually finished with this job.

That was when the light went on.

For several very good and quite logical reasons, Troy never carried a weapon while she was working. Even though, like Dallas, she was qualified as a sharpshooter with most handguns, she firmly believed that carrying a weapon bred a dependence on that rather than on her own wits. Also, and more importantly, her various law-enforcement supporters might not have been in favor of her efforts had they been worried by visions of guns going off through carelessness or panic. Besides, she didn't approve of violence.

Except in certain situations.

She turned quickly back to the room, her eyes adjusting to the light, and her mind clicked suddenly, belatedly, into gear. She ripped off her ski mask and then very calmly unclipped a Handie-Talkie from her tool belt and thumbed it on. "Jamie."

"Yes," he answered immediately, his voice whispering through the technological marvel she held in one hand.

Troy spoke evenly, her words edged with evidence of a growing rage. "We have been royally set up."

"Are you all right?" Jamie demanded quickly.

"Oh, I'm fine. You go on back; I'll be along later."

"But who—"

"Cameron," she answered briefly, interrupting his question. Then she switched off the Handie-Talkie and returned it to her belt. With barely controlled violence, not caring for the first time in her life about valuable and lovely works of art, she threw the chamois bag across the room. "I assume this is yours," she spit through gritted teeth. And it wasn't a question.

SIX

DALLAS CAUGHT THE pouch easily in one hand. He stepped from behind the reading chair in the corner and crossed to the desk, where he rested a hip on the edge and watched her gravely.

"I don't believe it," Troy said, her voice shaking with rage. "*I do not believe it*. It was all there, right under my nose and I didn't see it."

He waited silently, aware that she was, at the moment, more angry with herself than with him. The anger with him would come later.

Troy was pacing like a caged tigress. "A setup. And I walked right into it like a rank amateur. No *wonder* the security system was so lax: no *wonder* the house was conveniently empty." Even in the midst of her tirade Troy realized that there were conflicting emotions feeding her anger. She was angry with herself for having been too preoccupied to read the signs of a setup and furious with Dallas for making her feel like a fool. And since the latter anger could be safely vented, she let it have its way.

"And *you*." She whirled on him suddenly, her eyes glaring green fury. "How dare you do this to me! How *dare* you."

"I was trying to make a point," Dallas murmured, refusing to meet anger with anger.

"What point?" she demanded witheringly. "That I could be conned like three kinds of a fool?"

He ignored that. "Tell me, Troy. When I told you before that I didn't think what you do is wrong, did you believe me?"

"No," she snapped.

"And now?" he asked softly.

Troy stared at him, completely missing the point for a moment because of her anger. Then, slowly, she understood what he meant. "The money," she said dully. "The bonds, the jeweler's case. It was all a—a test, wasn't it?"

Dallas shook his head immediately. "No, it wasn't a test; I was proving a point. Troy, I knew damn well that you'd take only the figurine—"

"Was that other stuff supposed to tempt me?" she asked tightly.

"It would have tempted a *thief*," Dallas responded, "but you aren't a thief." He looked at her with a hint of pleading in his eyes. "I mistakenly called you a thief; I don't want that standing between us."

Determined to hang on to her anger at least long enough to air her grievances thoroughly, Troy ignored the plea. "This is your house, isn't it? Did you hire Chris Jordan to impersonate an anxious victim of theft?"

"He's a friend. Troy—"

"Is this your house?"

"Yes."

"And Roberts. The supposed thief? Another friend?"

"Yes—"

"Why couldn't we trace the deed to this house?"

"You aren't the only one with sources. I made sure the deed was temporarily misplaced."

Troy stared at him. "That's illegal."

"Isn't it though."

"Scrupulously legal Dallas Cameron illegally suppressing a deed?"

"You've turned me into a criminal," he said, suddenly mournful.

Totally against her will, she felt a laugh rising in her throat. The one perfect gem of Dallas's unlawful tampering had destroyed her temper as nothing else could have done.

Encouraged by her obvious amusement, Dallas continued along the same lines. "Between the two friends whom I was forced to take into my confidence and my source downtown, I've shot my lawful reputation all to hell. I'm sure it's only a matter of time before the gossip columns proclaim to the world that Cameron is tarnished beyond redemption."

She tried to conjure up a frown and failed. "You should be shot."

"You're not mad at me anymore, are you?"

"Of course, I'm mad. It was a low-down, underhanded, *sneaky* trick."

"Motivated by sheer desperation, I assure you."

"It didn't prove anything," Troy told him loftily. "I could have planned to come back later and empty the safe."

"Why?" Dallas asked reasonably. "The stuff in there is paltry compared to what you own yourself."

Troy stabbed a finger in his direction. "Ha! The truth will out. You decided that I wasn't a thief only because I obviously don't *need* to be a thief."

He looked thoughtful. "Partly that. But mostly because I've gotten to know you these last few days. You're no thief." When she made a slightly scornful noise, he added impulsively, "And I'm so sure of that, I'd consider it an honor to be your backup on your next job."

Troy started to laugh derisively at that, but she was reluctantly impressed by his willingness to participate in what he had—at least in the beginning—considered to be unlawful and morally wrong. "I thought you said that the edge of danger was a slippery place. Sure you want to walk on the edge?"

Dallas sighed softly. "One of these days, Miss

Bennett, you're going to realize that I have absolutely no sense of self-preservation where you're concerned. Shameful, but true. I will undoubtedly be ruthlessly blackmailed by two former friends for the remainder of my life because I was forced to bare my soul to them and confess an obsession for a benevolent cat burglar; I have taken my life in my hands—or in yours—each time I've gotten into that little black misguided missile laughingly called a car; and last, but by no means least, I seem to have developed the fixed intention of hitching my fate to a redheaded, half-French lady cat burglar who also happens to be a Rhodes Scholar, an electronics expert, a pilot, a pillar of Washington society, a philanthropist, a rather talented singer, and who happens to possess one of the most hair-trigger tempers I've ever encountered."

He took a deep breath, then added dryly, "In your estimation, Miss Bennett, does all of the above make me a reasonably sane, self-preserving male?"

"No." Troy was torn between laughter and bemusement.

"Then obviously I consider the slippery edge of danger to be just my kind of place."

She stared at him for a moment, then said suddenly, "I was supposed to be mad."

"Are you?"

"No."

"Good."

"You're a devious—"

"Hush," he interrupted severely. "You'll ruin my image of your ladylike self if you call me what I think you were about to call me."

"Ladylike?" Troy viewed him with real astonishment. "Are you trying to be funny?"

"Not at all. After much thought and very careful scrutiny, I've come to the conclusion that you, Miss Bennett, are what used to be termed a lady. The word has become rather shopworn, I'm afraid, so please understand that I mean it in the old-fashioned sense."

Troy leaned an elbow on the back of a nearby chair, inwardly pleased—though astonished—and trying not to show it. "I see. Thank you. Are you—in the old-fashioned sense—a gentleman?"

Dallas winced. "I was afraid you'd ask something like that."

"Well?"

He stared at her for a moment, then said slowly and quite calmly, "If I weren't at least some variation of a gentleman, Miss Bennett, I wouldn't be experiencing so many sleepless nights or taking quite so many cold showers. Because I would have tried my damnedest to—uh—coerce *you* to—uh—give in to that spark between us."

"That sounded like a very careful speech," Troy murmured.

"I'm glad you noticed."

"Of course, I noticed. I've also noticed your . . . restraint these last days."

"And?" he asked with an exaggerated puppy-dog-hopeful look.

"I commend you."

"Thanks a lot."

"Well?"

"Can't you do better than that?"

Troy gave him an innocent look. "Come now, Mr. Cameron. If I threw myself into your arms and—uh—wantonly gave in to that spark you mentioned, you could hardly continue thinking of me as a lady, could you?"

Dallas looked suddenly disgusted. "I seem to have boxed myself in."

"I'd say so."

He frowned for a moment, and then the frown abruptly cleared. "Ah—I have it. A change of strategy here."

"Yes?"

"Marry me."

Troy's mouth dropped open. She *knew* it was open, and she couldn't seem to do a damn thing about it. Dallas didn't appear to notice.

In the reasonable tone of one who'd found the solution to a difficult, tricky problem, he explained, "It's the best answer, you know. You will preserve your ladylike virtues in my eyes and I'll be able to go back to taking hot showers. I'm not so sure that I'll get any more sleep, but—"

"You're out of your mind," Troy said blankly.

"Now, *that* hurt," Dallas told her, clearly aggrieved.

Off-balance and totally flustered for one of the very few times in her life, Troy tried to make sense of her own thoughts. She hastily revised her earlier conclusions about obsession versus taking her home to meet Mother. Dallas was completely serious, and she knew it.

It was one of the most unnerving realizations she'd ever had. Almost inaudibly she murmured, "Dallas, I never said marriage or nothing...."

"I know you didn't," he interrupted calmly. "In fact, you said something along the lines of 'someone's going to have to get me pregnant first.' I'm entirely willing to trap you, you understand, but that method presents a hell of a conflict."

"Oh?" she managed weakly.

He nodded solemnly. "Since you're an old-fashioned lady, and I'm a variation of an old-fashioned gentleman, that method is actually ruled out from the start. Also I'm all for planned parenthood, and I'd really prefer to begin our marriage with two rather than three."

"Oh." She seemed addicted to the inane syllable.

"So I think"—Dallas remained solemn and reasonable "—that my idea is best."

"Uh...oh?" *Great variations on the one-syllable theme, Troy!* she thought in self-disgust.

"Yes. Marry me."

Troy managed somehow to shake off the spell.

"Is that a command or a proposal?" she de-manded, her voice not nearly as angry as she would have liked.

Very softly Dallas said, "Am I the only one who's suffered these past days, Troy? Am I the only one who's spent sleepless nights after cold showers?" His voice deepened suddenly. "Do you wake up in the middle of the night the way I do, aching inside? Do you toss and turn in your lonely bed the way I do, with nothing to hold on to?"

She turned away suddenly, going over to the fireplace and staring blindly up at the lithograph hung above the mantel. His questions were echo-ing inside of her, torturing her with the promise of what could be. Didn't he realize what he was do-ing to her? Troy asked herself.

As if he'd read her mind, Dallas answered the unspoken question.

"Can't you see what we're doing to each other? Dammit, I know I promised not to pressure you, but I can't take much more of this, Troy."

"You said you just wanted to get to know me," she told him almost inaudibly. "You promised. An empty promise?"

"Troy...."

Slowly, reluctantly, drawn by the plea in his voice, she turned to face him. And she saw something in his eyes that stopped her heart.

"The promise was made in good faith," he said gently. "But I've discovered that...love isn't a very patient demon."

Her heart began to beat again, slowly, heavily, its rhythm unsteady. Her feet were rooted to the floor, her body frozen. She wanted to question the word, the emotion, but couldn't somehow. It hung there between them, suspended in midair by disbelief. Troy swallowed hard and fastened onto another word, one she could say aloud. "Demon?"

Dallas set the chamois bag down neatly in the center of his desk, then crossed the room to stand in front of her. "Demon," he murmured. "A persistently tormenting person, force, or passion. In this case, all three. You're my demon, Troy. And the love I feel for you is a force and a passion too strong to fight."

"You barely know me," she whispered.

"I know enough." His hands lifted to rest on her shoulders, as if he needed to touch her. Blue eyes looked down at her with an honesty that she could not question. "I know that you could easily belong to a careless, jet-setting crowd, interested in nothing but your own pleasure—but you don't. You pack more hours into a week than it was ever meant to hold, and you spend those hours helping people. You love children and animals, and they love you. You have a quick temper, a quick laugh—and a quick tongue."

He was smiling down at her with an odd, whimsical tenderness. "You're vulnerable on one hand because you care for people, and cynical on the other hand because you've learned the empty value of empty promises." His smile faded, the blue eyes probing. "And you're not afraid of love, but for some reason, you're afraid of loving...me."

Troy stared up at him, silently marveling because he was totally comfortable with his own masculinity; so much so that he could admit love without hesitation or excuses, but with an odd kind of freedom she only vaguely understood. She looked at the strikingly handsome face and felt a surge of hope that no amount of reason could dispel.

"Why are you afraid of loving me, Troy?"

She tried to ignore the hope, tried to use reason. "It's impossible."

"Nothing is impossible," he told her fiercely, his hands tightening on her shoulders.

"*This is!*" she cried.

"Why? Dammit, why is it so impossible?"

"Because if I love you, you'll take over!" Dimly Troy wondered if she was making sense; she pushed on because something was driving her to say it all now and get it over with. "I won't be in control of my life anymore! You'll ask me to give up at least a part of my work, and because I love you, I'll give it up. And that's wrong—*wrong*."

"Because you love me," he murmured very softly.

For a moment Troy thought that he had heard only that, but then she realized that he had heard everything—even what she had not meant to say. She tried to step back, but his hands wouldn't release her. A little voice inside her head sneered at her for being unable to say except by accident that she loved him.

"I needed to hear that," he said. There was a small, raw flame in his blue eyes. "Because now I *know* it isn't impossible. Now I know we can make it work."

"Dallas—"

He cut her off quickly, determined to say what he felt so strongly. "Troy, you're afraid that I'll use your love, that I'll use emotional blackmail to force you to give up the part of your work we both know I'm uncomfortable with. Yes?"

She nodded silently.

"I won't," he said flatly.

Troy stared at him for a moment, and then stepped back; this time he didn't stop her. She began wandering aimlessly around the room, needing the space and the activity to help her think. Evenly she said, "We'll play Let's Pretend for a moment, all right?"

"All right." He was watching her intently.

"Let's pretend we—we get married."

Dallas nodded silently, realizing that this was not the time to respond to her words with a wholehearted "Let's not pretend; let's do it!" even though it was what he wanted to say.

"Now I average going out at night on a job about twice a month. Could you live with that?"

"I'd have to, wouldn't I?" he answered quietly.

Troy shot him a quick, searching look. "What about if we decided to start a family?"

"You wouldn't go out on a job; your own common sense would prevent you," he said in a tone of absolute certainty.

She looked at him again, then absently unfastened the heavy tool belt and dropped it on the desk as she paced past. "During pregnancy, you're right," she said. "What about after?"

Dallas hesitated. "You're crossing bridges before we come to them."

"I have to." She stopped, swinging around to face him. "I have to, Dallas. Because once we begin, there's no going back. I don't believe that marriages should end up in divorce court, and I don't think you do either."

"*We* won't end up there, Troy."

"Famous last words," she said bleakly.

In two quick steps he stood before her again, swiftly pulling her against him. His arms were hard, yet gentle, holding her in an embrace meant to comfort, to reassure. "Sweetheart, don't do this to yourself," he said huskily. "Don't you understand that the most important thing in the world to me is that you be happy?" He fumbled for words, trying desperately to make her see that it simply wasn't in him to deny her anything— even things that hurt him or made him fear for her. "I would never ask you to be less than you are."

Troy took a deep breath, the cool, spicy scent of his cologne sending her senses into a dizzy spin. "What about those two million years of instinct you mentioned earlier?" she whispered.

"I'll fight the instinct. Although," he added wryly, "I don't expect it to be easy. You'll have to help me, sweetheart. And you'll have to be patient with me."

The warmth spreading through her, Troy realized dimly, was a combination of several things. The oddly tender endearment that sounded new on his lips. The security of his embrace. The love and understanding she could feel in him. Her own love rising up within her in spite of her inner attempts to deny it.

She allowed her cheek to rest against his chest, suddenly tired and sleepy and completely unable to fight. Her eyelids felt made of lead and only his arms held her upright. *Nature's restorative*, she decided drowsily, *is sleep. And I think I'll have some*....

"Troy?" he murmured into her hair.

"Mmm?"

"Marry me?"

"Mmm...."

She felt herself drifting away. From a very great distance she heard a rumbling sound that might have been a rueful laugh, but it didn't trouble her. She was so tired....

The ceiling was unfamiliar. It was the first thing Troy saw when she reluctantly opened one eye, and she stared up at it for a long moment in puzzlement. The light fixture was all wrong. And everything was too bright; her bedroom had a western exposure because she strongly disliked morning sun.

She forced her other eye open and continued to study the ceiling. No...still wrong. That wasn't her ceiling. Lazily Troy considered her position, which was on her back in a very comfortable bed. Thick covers cocooned her in warmth, the arm across her stomach anchoring them in place.

Arm?

Troy pulled her arms out from under the covers; the weight across her stomach remained. Lifting her head, she craned to see that it was a decidedly masculine arm across her middle.

Without moving a muscle, reluctant to look sideways and find out to whom the arm was attached, she carefully went over in her mind the events of the night before. Everything fell into place, except—Was she in Dallas's bed? And had she really fallen asleep more or less in the middle of his proposal?

Troy winced and let her head fall back on the pillow. She was completely dressed except for her kid boots; she must have been dead tired, because she was always uncomfortable in bed unless she slept in the buff. As it was, awareness of her clothing was making her acutely uncomfortable now.

She lay still for a moment, debating the best way to handle this. She was amazingly clear-headed after the needed sleep and, though still bemused by the events of last night, she felt much less certain than she had before that the barriers between Dallas and her were insurmountable.

If—*if*—Dallas could live with her work, they just might have a chance. The thought made her smile happily, inside and out. Some of her sparring partner's determination seemed to have rubbed off on her; she was quite suddenly aware of a fierce intention to give this relationship every chance possible.

But there was still a cautious part of her that wanted to be sure of at least a reasonable possibility of success. So if Dallas didn't strangle her for falling asleep at a rather inopportune moment... well, they'd just have to see what could be worked out.

In the meantime, Troy mused, what could she do to make things easier on both of them? It occurred belatedly to her that she'd been taking herself far too seriously—professionally and personally. She had a sense of humor, dammit. Was Dallas even *aware* of that?

It also occurred to her that for a woman who'd never in her life awakened in a man's bed, she was taking it very well. Troy grinned inwardly, got her priorities in order, then rose on an elbow and gazed down at Dallas.

He was lying on his stomach beside her,

stripped to the waist at least—she didn't care to speculate further—with his face nuzzled into her pillow so that only one closed eye was visible beneath a shock of raven hair. Troy gave in to impulse and gently brushed the lock of hair back, then politely tapped on his tanned shoulder.

"Hello?"

The eye opened blearily and focused on her elbow, which was resting some inches from his nose. It was a very puzzled eye.

"Hello," Troy repeated brightly.

Dallas lifted his head immediately, the other eye opening and joining its fellow in looking extremely puzzled. The lock of hair fell gently back over his forehead, lending him an endearingly boyish look not a whit marred by the morning stubble that darkened his jaw. And in his bleary eyes was the shell-shocked expression of a late riser forced to stir at dawn.

Troy swallowed a giggle; if he was always this reluctant to wake up, she thought, the past few days of "tagging along" with her at the crack of dawn must have been sheer hell for him!

"Are you there?" she demanded.

"No," he mumbled, pushing himself up on an

elbow so as to be able to smother a huge yawn without removing his arm from across her waist. "I'll be here in a minute."

"Well, while you're getting here, d'you mind if I take a shower? I hate sleeping in my clothes."

"S'fine with me," he managed, yawning again.

"Well?"

He winced. "Don't throw questions like that at me in my condition. Well, what?"

"Does the referee have to ring the bell?" When he only stared at her blankly, she swallowed a giggle and elaborated. "You've got me pinned down here."

"Ah."

"Yes."

"So I have." His eyes were clearing.

"You have to move before I can." She frowned suddenly. "And I'd better call home. The last thing Jamie heard from me was a raging temper; he probably thinks I've killed you by now."

"I called him last night."

Troy stared at him. "Clever of you to remember that."

"I told you I was getting here."

"Mmm. Well, if you wouldn't mind moving..."

Quite suddenly, Dallas moved. He hauled her closer to him—almost beneath him—and kissed her. Several times.

Before Troy could regain her breath or do more than wonder how her arms had ended up around his neck, he was speaking in a calm voice devoid of any trace of sleep.

"I have also just remembered that you fell asleep in the middle of my proposal."

"Sorry about that," she murmured.

Dallas addressed the ceiling. "Sorry, she says. *Sorry.* My ego is in absolute tatters, not to mention my heart, and she says sorry. The woman has no sense of decency. Does she fling her arms around my neck and tearfully apologize?"

"My arms are around your neck," she pointed out reprovingly.

He ignored that. "No, she just says sorry about that. Sorry about that, Dallas, but it's raining. Sorry about that, Dallas, the laundry left a spot on your shirt. Sorry about that, Dallas, but the Chinese takeout place forgot the egg rolls."

Troy was giggling helplessly. "Enough! Did it

ever occur to you that it wasn't my response but your timing that was at fault?"

"What was wrong with my timing?" he demanded, injured.

"It was definitely off. Now, may I please be allowed to go take a shower?"

"Do I get an answer to my proposal?"

"Not until I've had a shower and coffee." Troy looked thoughtful. "And breakfast."

"You believe in being fortified, don't you?" he asked wryly.

"For all of life's major decisions—certainly."

With deliberate lightness Dallas asked, "Does that mean you're at least considering it seriously?"

Troy matched his tone. "I always take proposals seriously. I found out the hard way that it saves trouble in the end."

"How'd you find that out?" Dallas released her and remained propped on his elbow as he watched her slide from the bed.

She stood beside the bed and grimaced faintly as she looked down at the supposedly no-wrinkle material, which had wrinkled during the night. Running her fingers through her hair in a quick repair job, she answered his question reflectively.

"Well, I was in North Africa once, and this Arab—robes and everything—more or less ordered me to become his wife. He was speaking Arabic, but—"

"You speak Arabic?" Dallas interrupted.

"A smattering. Enough to know what he was talking about. Anyway, I said something flippant like 'Ready anytime you are, Clyde.' The next day, the embassy was in an uproar because this guy—who turned out to be a sheikh—sent *herds* of camels and goats to buy me." When Dallas burst out laughing, she frowned down at him. "Don't laugh; it took weeks to convince Clyde to go shopping somewhere else."

"You should put a lid on that charm of yours!" Dallas laughed.

"It had nothing to do with charm," Troy said firmly. "It was my hair. Arabs are fascinated by blondes and redheads. Which way to the shower, please? You may remember that I was somewhat out of it last night and missed the guided tour. By the way, how did I get here?"

Dallas sat up in bed and linked his arms loosely around his upraised knees. "I carried you."

"And I missed that?" Troy mourned. "Damn. I always wanted to be swept off my feet."

"I'll make a note of it," he said thoughtfully. "And the master bath is through those doors over there. Towels, soap, shampoo, toothpaste, and a new toothbrush are in the linen closet. Help yourself."

"I'll do that."

"And I'll try to scrounge fresh clothes for you."

Troy stopped at the doors and turned to face him, lifting an eyebrow. Do you keep clothes here for your women? Nothing of yours would fit."

"For your information," he told her calmly, "no woman other than my sister has spent the night here since I've owned the place. But I believe she left a pair of jeans here." Mockingly stern, he warned, "And if you want breakfast, you'd better stop jumping to conclusions."

Troy bowed with exaggerated obeisance and Dallas threw a pillow at her.

"Take your shower," he directed, "before I decide to drown you for going to sleep on me last night."

Laughing, Troy disappeared into the bathroom.

Dallas looked after her for a moment with a smile, then threw back the covers and got out of bed. He wondered vaguely if she realized that he'd spent the better part of the night gazing at her as she lay sleeping in his bed.

SEVEN

TROY STEPPED UNDER a steaming hot shower in the large bathroom, resisting the temptation of a tub deep enough to swim in and boasting every modern convenience. She automatically washed her hair, swearing softly when she remembered where she was; hopefully Dallas owned a dryer. The thought of where she was also caused her to turn the water ice-cold before she stepped out, shivering, onto the mat.

She reached for a large towel, muttering to herself. He'd been right, dammit; cold showers were no fun at all. She watched goose bumps rise on her arms, wondering if they were caused by the cold water or by her memory of just how hard it had been to leave his bed.

She wrapped her hair in a second towel and was just about to start yelling for Dallas when he tapped on the door.

"Clothes on the bed," he called in a muffled voice. "And breakfast downstairs when you're ready. Just follow your nose."

"Hey! D'you have a hair dryer?"

"Top shelf of the linen closet."

"Thanks."

"Sure. I'm going to take a shower myself; meet you downstairs."

"Okay."

Locating the hair dryer, Troy plugged it in and dried her hair, borrowing his comb to style it loosely. She put everything away neatly when she was finished, whistling softly to herself. Then, wearing only her towel, she opened the bathroom door and breezed out into the bedroom.

And stopped dead.

The woman was tall, slender, raven-haired— and gorgeous. She was casually dressed in slacks and a sweater that showed off every eye-stopping inch of a figure that Venus would have killed for. Her profile was toward Troy as she stood with hands on hips and stared at the rumpled bed bearing unmistakable signs of two occupants: two headprints on the pillow (Dallas had thrown his pillow at her, and it still lay on the floor by the bathroom doors), and the covers thrown back from both sides of the bed.

For a moment—a single, eternal moment—Troy took in the woman's presence in Dallas's bedroom and felt a heart-jolting stab of jealousy.

But then the woman turned to face her, and Troy relaxed. Torn between amusement and embarrassment at her sketchy attire, she said a little wryly, "Hi, I'm Troy Bennett."

"Hi," the brunette responded in an equally wry tone. "I'm Andrea Cameron." Her dark blue eyes laughed suddenly. "I came for my jeans, but I think you need them more than I do!"

Dallas's sister was twenty-six years old, a buyer for a rather famous antique dealer, and every bit as brilliant as she was beautiful. She was also completely delighted to have found Troy wrapped in a towel in her brother's bedroom. And as she and Troy sat together in the dining room drinking coffee and waiting for Dallas before eating breakfast, she told Troy exactly *why* she was so delighted.

"He was always so damn *perfect*," she explained cheerfully, her lovely contralto voice wry. "Not stuffy; I don't mean that. It's just that Dallas never took a wrong step. Maybe it was because he's the oldest, I don't know. But it drove Tony and me *crazy* when we were kids; we gave up on the sibling rivalry bit before we reached high school. I mean, what was the *point?*"

Troy was trying not to laugh. "That doesn't explain why you're so delighted to find me here. What is it—how the mighty are fallen?"

Andrea laughed. "More like sauce for the goose. Ever since he moved his home office here to D.C., he's been watching over me like a hen with one chick! Up until a week or so ago, that is, and I'm betting that's when you two met."

Nodding, Troy understood exactly what the younger woman was getting at.

Andrea chuckled softly. "That's it. I have a feeling he'll be too busy to worry about me—at least for a while."

Troy studied her speculatively, saying suddenly, "I have a friend you really should meet."

"Male, I hope?" Andrea lifted a brow.

"Definitely, and I think you two would be perfect for each other. I have to warn you, though, he's slippery as an eel."

Andrea pursed her lips thoughtfully, her blue eyes laughing. "A runner, huh? How far and how fast?"

"He'll probably break the record for the cross-country dash," Troy said solemnly.

"Mmm. Sounds like a lot of work. Is he worth it?"

"Tom Elliot."

Andrea sat up straighter. "The blond god with the voice of pure honey? That Tom Elliot?"

"That's him."

Hitching her chair closer to Troy, Andrea said in a briskly conspiratorial tone, "Give me the lowdown on the course, friend. What kind of hurdles do I expect, and what's my competition?"

They were laughing together in perfect understanding and in an entirely feminine way when Dallas walked into the room a few moments later. He looked startled, but clearly not irritated by his sister's presence. His gaze took in the two women and their air of conspiracy, noting along the way how well Andrea's jeans and sweater fit Troy.

He bent to kiss his sister's cheek before heading for his chair. "Morning, Andy."

"Morning." Andrea sat back and sent him a mock-baleful stare. "Should I read you the sisterly riot act now, or save it for later?"

"The riot act?" He sat down and unfolded his napkin, smiling. "What have I done this time?"

Andrea summoned a scandalized tone. "You've only abducted this poor child and held her against her will in your villainous abode—*all night*! She's ruined, you brute!"

Dallas sighed. "Before I repeat something I've said constantly over the years, just let me observe that it'd take a hell of a lot more than one night of sin to ruin Troy Bennett. I think she's invincible."

Troy waved her fork for attention and hastily swallowed the bite of fruit she'd just taken. "Hey! You siblings stop discussing my reputation, will you, please? And it wasn't a night of sin."

"Passion, then," Dallas murmured.

"You're giving your sister the wrong idea," Troy told him severely. She looked at Andrea gravely. "We were—uh—having a discussion last night, and I fell asleep on him."

Andrea choked on her juice, turning watering eyes to her brother. "You'll have to polish up your prose style."

Dallas winced. "I'll definitely repeat what I've said constantly over the years: Sisters should be strangled at birth."

The housekeeper entering the room with bacon and eggs prevented Andrea from retorting in kind, but her look at Dallas was full of awful promise.

"Troy, did my graceless sister introduce you to my housekeeper, Mrs. Bradley?"

"Yes, I did." Andrea said indignantly.

Troy smiled a little at Mrs. Bradley, resisting an impulse to respond to the laugh in her merry brown eyes. The middle-aged housekeeper seemed entirely accustomed to these two Camerons, and their amiable verbal fencing matches.

As the housekeeper left the room, Andrea got to her feet with an insulted "And if you're going to pick on me, I'm going home."

Dallas smiled gently at her.

Hastily Troy said, "I'll send your clothes back tomorrow, Andrea, if that's okay."

Andrea pointedly ignored her brother. "That's fine, Troy. Oh, and—give me a call next week about you-know-who."

"Right."

"Who?" Dallas demanded when his sister had gone.

Troy thoughtfully crunched bacon, taking her time. "None of your business," she said mildly.

He sighed. "I think my future comfort would be more assured if you and my sister *didn't* get along so well," he observed.

"Tough luck," Troy commiserated.

Peace reigned for a while—but just a short while. Troy realized only a few moments later that, breakfast and casual conversation aside, Dallas was watching her like a hawk.

She placed her fork neatly on her plate and stared at him across the table.

"Something wrong?" Dallas wanted to know.

"You tell me."

"Come again?"

"You've been staring at me. I was just wondering why."

"Well, you've nearly finished breakfast, haven't you?"

"And so?"

"How soon we forget. My proposal."

"Oh. That."

Dallas propped an elbow on the table and rested his forehead in his hand in a gesture of despair. "People who invite pain," he murmured, "have always puzzled me. Until now. I think I'm turning into a masochist."

Severely Troy said, "Well, any man who makes a proposal of marriage in the tone of a business deal deserves everything he gets!"

Brightening, Dallas raised his head and tossed his napkin aside. "Is that the problem? Hell, why didn't you say so sooner?" He stood and came around to her chair, pulling it out slightly, and then went down quite calmly on one knee.

He should have looked ridiculous...but he didn't. Troy gazed down at him and felt her heart flutter. She didn't resist when he took both her hands in his, dimly realizing that if he'd used this tactic last night, the bed they had shared might have been a far cry from platonic.

"Dallas..."

"Marry me, sweetheart." He lifted her hands to his lips, kissing each one in turn. "Please. I love you so much."

From the corner of her eye Troy saw the door to the kitchen start to open and then swing quickly shut as Mrs. Bradley clearly decided not to intrude. If Dallas saw, it obviously didn't bother him.

She looked at him and wondered again at his willingness to be vulnerable, his openness in expressing his feelings. Without conscious thought, her right hand freed itself and lifted to touch his cheek, feeling the smoothness of his skin, feeling a knot of tension in his jaw.

Dallas reached into a pocket of his slacks with his free hand, removing a small black velvet box. He thumbed the catch open, his eyes never leaving her face, to reveal a glittering marquise diamond engagement ring. "Marry me," he said softly, fiercely.

Troy looked at the ring and then his face. "I want to," she whispered. "But I can't promise, Dallas. It's too soon."

He took a slow, deep breath. "Will you wear the ring?" When she hesitated, he added gently,

"It's not a promise, Troy; I just want to know you're wearing it."

She nodded and watched gravely as he slid the ring onto her fourth finger. It fit perfectly. She managed a shaky smile. "Such odd times you choose to propose. First last night after I broke into your house, and now this morning over breakfast."

"I'll have to choose moonlight and romance the next time," he vowed thoughtfully, rising to his feet and pulling her gently up. Her reluctance to commit herself didn't appear to disturb him unduly. He smiled down at her whimsically. "And while we're discussing odd things, d'you think you could spare the time this week to be abducted?"

Troy found herself torn between laughter and tears. "What?"

"Abducted. As in I sling you over my saddle and ride off into the desert. Remember the sheikh who wanted to buy you? I want to steal you for a few days."

Troy couldn't help it; she started laughing. "Why don't you just borrow me for a while?" she gasped.

He frowned at her reprovingly. "I'm serious. D'you think Jamie could hold down the fort without you for a while?"

"Why?"

"Because," he said, "I'd like you to myself a little while. For a couple of reasons."

"Which are?" she inquired warily.

"You're tired, sweetheart. You need a break from that mad dash you do every day. And I'd like for us to spend some time together with only each other for company. We could stay here—or go somewhere, if you'd rather. But I think we need the time, Troy."

Troy, knowing very well that their sporadic time alone together was the major reason they'd not yet become lovers, wondered if he knew what he was doing. Being Troy, she asked him.

"Do you know what you're doing?"

He grinned slightly. "I think I'm waving a lighted match at dynamite."

Calmly Troy said, "Well, just so you know."

He gave her a bemused stare. "You'll stay?"

"You're more polite than the sheikh. I'll stay."

"No demands up front for separate bedrooms?"

"You're a gentleman—remember?"

"Damn. I knew I'd boxed myself in with that one."

"Uh-huh."

Dallas smiled wryly. "Well, at least you're staying."

"Yes. But in case you've forgotten the benefit's tonight. And since it's formal, I don't think your sister's jeans and sweater will fit the bill. I'll have to go home—or send home—for clothes."

"Send home," he said immediately. "I don't trust Jamie not to talk you into changing your mind."

"Jamie gave up on trying to change my mind about anything years ago," she told him dryly.

Dallas shook his head slightly, then had a sudden thought. "This benefit tonight?"

"What about it?"

"I just hope to hell you haven't planned on another escort."

"Besides you, you mean?" She smiled oddly. "No. But you may live to regret it."

He looked down at her warily. "Why?"

"The gossip columnists will be out in force, and both of us are sirloin for their meat grinders." Troy had a sudden thought of her own, lifting her left hand and staring at the engagement ring. "And they're sure to spot this."

Dallas looked at her steadily.

She returned the stare for a moment, then shrugged recklessly. "What the hell. I don't care if you don't."

He relaxed visibly. "Then neither of us cares. Come on: you can call home for clothes and then I'll give you the guided tour."

The guided tour showed off a truly beautiful home. The furnishings were an eclectic mixture of comfortable modern pieces and priceless antiques, with several really good paintings and lithographs, and lovely collections of jade and ivory.

It was a large house for a single man, but Troy didn't have to be told that Dallas did a fair amount of business entertaining. Still, there seemed an excessive number of bedrooms—until Dallas explained.

"I'd love to fill these with kids," he said casually, waving a hand toward a hall filled with currently unoccupied rooms.

Troy stopped abruptly and stared up at him. "That's a tall order."

"Not really," he told her serenely. "Twins run in my family."

She continued to stare at him, finally asking in a careful tone, "Any other little surprises you'd like to spring on me?"

He reflected. "Not at the moment."

"Thanks." Troy sighed. "I just may live to fight another day."

"I'm counting on it, sweetheart."

Jamie arrived about the time the tour concluded, bearing with him the requested clothes and arriving in his own large sedan, since he always refused to drive Troy's little Porsche. He remained for coffee, subjecting neither of them to questions, but both to a benevolent stare that made Dallas more than a little uncomfortable— and Jamie didn't say a word about the diamond. He left about an hour later, calmly assuring Troy that he'd take care of the business until she chose to return, and giving Dallas a handshake that was firm without—quite—breaking bones.

Dallas massaged his hand as he shut the door behind the big man, sending Troy a pained glance. "He doesn't know his own strength."

"Oh, yes he does." Troy smiled gently. "To the last ounce."

"Have I been warned?" Dallas demanded.

"Sorry about that. Jamie is a bit overprotective sometimes."

"He looked intimidating."

"He always looks that way."

"I thought you said that if you wanted a watch-dog, you'd buy a Doberman?"

"I didn't have a choice with Jamie."

The day was spent with relative calm compared to the hectic pace Troy normally maintained. And it was a peculiar day in many ways. They were virtually alone; Mrs. Bradley never appeared except during lunch. The phone never once rang, prompting Troy's conclusion that Dallas had warned his office not to disturb him.

So they were alone. And since the sparkling diamond on her finger was a constant reminder to Troy of just how serious Dallas was about her, she found herself looking at him and responding to him in a new way. She spent most of the day rather puzzled though; while his eyes were warm and caressing whenever they rested on her, Dallas seemed to be avoiding any physical contact.

The logical reason for that, of course, occurred to Troy, but instead of being glad that he'd apparently decided not to pressure her, she found herself expressing quite a few decidedly *un*ladylike sentiments to herself.

He really didn't have to keep *that* much distance between them, she thought irritably. He'd said that he loved her; It certainly wasn't evident by his touch-me-not attitude. Troy knew that she was being unreasonable again, and realized quite sanely that she couldn't have it both ways. The spark between them was just waiting for kindling to feed its hunger, and the simplest of touches could easily start the fire.

But Troy, restlessly watching him whenever she thought he wasn't looking, wasn't willing to be reasonable. Over a chessboard late that afternoon she stared at his hand as it hovered ready to move a piece and she remembered the touch of that hand when they'd danced together in her library. She recalled the curious feeling of suspended reality during that interlude and quite suddenly wanted to feel that again.

She wanted Dallas. Admitting it silently brought a rush of feverish intensity through her body, and an odd breathless dizziness. She felt shocked, painfully aware of him as she'd never been before.

"Check," he said cheerfully, moving a piece decisively and then looking across the board at her. They were sitting comfortably on the carpet on either side of the big glass-topped coffee table in his large den, a fire blazing merrily in the stone hearth just a few feet away. Only the crackle of the flames broke the sudden silence.

"I . . . concede," Troy said slowly, in a voice that seemed to her unfamiliar.

Dallas stared across at her, the golden, feverish intensity of her eyes holding him as if by a spell. She was looking at him, he thought, as if she'd never seen him before, the sudden awareness in her eyes a naked thing. "Troy?" he breathed huskily, questioning what he couldn't put into words.

She reached out slowly, without taking her eyes off him, to tip her king over in acknowledgment of defeat. "I . . . concede," she repeated softly.

And then, before either of them could move or speak again, the antique grandfather clock out in the hall announced the hour with the whirring, rasping sound of gallant old age. It was six o'clock.

Blindly Troy looked down at her watch. "We should get ready for the benefit," she murmured. "There's a dinner and dancing first, then the performance."

"Your things were put in the master bedroom," Dallas said, wanting to say something else. "I moved some of mine to the bedroom across the hall. You go on up: I'll put the board away."

Troy rose to her feet in silence and left the room, afraid to look at him again because she knew she wouldn't be able to leave him even momentarily if she did.

She went up to the master bedroom, where they'd spent the night, her movements automatic. She took a shower and, wrapped in a towel, applied makeup and arranged her hair on top of her head in a deceptively casual style with loose strands framing her face. She dabbed on a small amount of her favorite perfume and placed diamond studs in her earlobes. Then she stepped into the bedroom to stare at the dress lying across the king-size bed.

The dress had been chosen for tonight days

ago, but Troy wondered vaguely if she'd had some idea of starting a fire even then. Of all her wardrobe this dress had the best chance of being labeled combustible. She'd bought it in Paris, but she'd never had the nerve to wear it before and wasn't sure she did tonight.

It was fashioned from a gold material that shimmered with every breath, until it seemed almost to breathe on its own. Fastened in a very flimsy knot on one shoulder and leaving the other shoulder bare, the material displayed little more flesh than most of her evening gowns. But, defying every law of gravity and not relying on strategically placed darts, the material draped seductively over her breasts, leaving her back almost bare, and clung to her hips and thighs. There was a slit up the right side almost to her hip, and it was absolutely impossible to wear anything underneath it.

Troy took a deep breath and determinedly got into the dress, deciding to leave whatever outcome there might be in the hands of the gods. Avoiding a long look in the mirror, she slid her feet into gold pumps and picked up her clutch and white fur jacket, then went downstairs.

Holding her purse and jacket in one hand, she used the other to pick up the long skirt as she carefully descended the stairs. She was paying complete attention to what she was doing and didn't realize that Dallas was standing at the bottom watching her until he spoke.

"A flame," he murmured huskily just as she reached the second step. "A beautiful, sexy flame. They say that one of man's greatest accomplishments was the discovery of fire. But the fire was there all along, in woman. Especially you, sweetheart. You were born fire."

"And what were you born?" she asked, wondering dimly at the throaty sound of her own voice, wondering how he could possibly look so shatteringly handsome dressed in stark black.

Dallas smiled slowly. "Judging by the way I feel, I was born wood." His voice deepened suddenly. "And we'd better get out of here before I set the house on fire."

Silently, conscious of an inner trembling she'd felt only once before, Troy stepped off the final stair and accepted his help in sliding into her jacket. They went out into the chilly evening air and got into the Mercedes, which he'd thought-fully warmed, and started the drive across town.

The benefit was for a children's organization, and was being held in a large hotel. Washington society had turned out in force, and so had the press. Flashbulbs and strobes were going con-stantly, and questions—business, political, or just gossipy—were shouted at the guests as they arrived.

Having run the gauntlet outside, there was a second one of friends and acquaintances inside, and it was nearly half an hour before Troy and Dallas managed to reach their table. Along the way they'd encountered speculative looks and arch questions, which both had ignored for the simple reason that they were only marginally aware of anything but each other.

A barely audible voice in Troy's head told her that she was wearing her heart on her sleeve for all the world to see, but she couldn't stop gazing at Dallas. The bottomless depths of his blue eyes fascinated her; the way the taut flesh molded itself over the fine bones of his face fascinated her; the way he moved, the sound of his voice—all these fascinated her.

Dallas, who'd been fascinated and captivated from the beginning, could wish only that they were alone as he drank in the sight of Troy wearing a new and totally feminine hat. This Troy was one he'd searched for and hoped for since the beginning, and he was elated to have found her at last.

All through dinner they talked little, wrapped in their own world. The tension grew until it was quivering in the air between them. They ate what was put in front of them without noticing, heard the tumult of voices around them without listening. And when dinner was over and the music began for dancing, they rose with one mind.

It wasn't enough, Troy thought as she slipped into his arms on the handkerchief-size dance floor, just to touch. Moments earlier the thought of touching him had seemed heaven, but now it was hell. She couldn't be close enough to him, and to be only this close was torture. With arms around his neck her hands helplessly, compulsively stroked his thick black hair. She rested her cheek against the material of his jacket, stunningly aware of his breath softly stirring her hair and his hand resting like a brand of promise on the bare flesh of her back.

One dance, two, three—all in silence. They danced only the slow dances, and the seductive beat of the music seemed to enter Troy's veins and pounded in her heart. She lost all track of time, and when Tom came by their table to collect her for the songs they were doing together, she very nearly asked him what he was talking about. But reluctantly she went with him. Neither she nor Dallas had said a word in nearly an hour.

She accompanied Tom into the curtained-off area beside the small stage, wishing with a small and distant part of her mind that they'd been able to rehearse here instead of having been forced to use the concert hall. But it didn't really bother her. Nothing bothered her.

Tom brought her slightly back to earth.

"I'm happy for you, Blondie." He gestured toward the diamond, smiling slightly. "And I'll be even happier if you remember we're supposed to be singing together out there."

Troy blinked at him, then smiled. "I remember."

"Good. You shouldn't have any problems. They're love songs."

"You've been a good friend, Tommy," she told him seriously.

He looked alarmed. "Hey! We won't stop being friends just because Cameron finally found a way to catch you, will we? Or is he the jealous type?"

She shook her head ruefully. "I did sound as if I were about to abandon everything, didn't I? I think I've gone over the edge, Tommy."

"I know damn well you have," Tom said definitely, then winked at her and strolled out on stage as the master of ceremonies announced his name.

Troy listened absently as Tom joked with the audience for a few moments, then squared her shoulders and stepped out onto the stage when he introduced his partner for the evening.

Odd, she thought. She didn't even have butterflies.

Troy didn't remember very much of the performance when she looked back on it later. She remembered that the audience seemed pleased, and she remembered that she had no difficulty in locating Dallas in the crowd out front. She remembered singing directly to him because, as Tommy had said, they were love songs.

The rest of the evening stretched into an eternity. There were other performers she barely heard. There were more dances danced in silence. There were blue eyes across the table.

And then there were good nights and a silent drive across town in the Mercedes, and she realized that she didn't even mind being driven by him. The night was cold and crisp, and there was a full moon made just to order for them. The house was quiet because Mrs. Bradley had gone and dim because only a few lights had been left on.

And perhaps she was an old-fashioned kind of lady, as Dallas had said, but even old-fashioned ladies could let down their hair when the door was closed and the world shut out. Even old-fashioned ladies could love and be loved. And there was nothing—nothing at all—wrong with that.

Troy waited silently as Dallas removed her purse from nerveless fingers and laid it on a hall table before sliding the fur jacket off and placing it there also. Something tapped at the back of her mind as he turned back to her, the blue fire in his eyes reminding her of a slight misunderstanding that really needed to be cleared up.

"Dallas . . . about all those lovers in my past—"

Suddenly, with an odd, controlled violence, Dallas reached out and hauled her against his hard body, the flame in his eyes blazing higher and hotter. Something leaped out at her from those blue fires for a moment, something wild and primitive, and the rawness of it shocked and compelled.

"I don't want to hear, Troy," he vowed fiercely, his head bending toward hers. "Not now. I don't want to know—"

EIGHT

"Dallas—"

"I don't want to know," he repeated urgently, his lips seeking and finding hers in a demanding firestorm of need.

Troy dismissed the subject from her mind. Her fingers locked in his hair as her mouth came alive beneath his, matching searing desire with her own burning passion, setting alight a fire that could never be put out. She felt the starkly possessive invasion of his tongue as her own dueled with his in the instinctive hunger of the ages.

The tremors that had shaken her all evening

spread outward now, from the core of her being, like ripples in a pool. She was hot, then cold; strong, then weak. Colors whirled wildly behind her closed eyelids and every nerve ending seemed sensitized almost beyond bearing. Only his lips on hers smothered the cry of pleasure aching to escape when his hand slid probingly up her spine. Her body arched into his compulsively, and her desire spiraled suddenly into frantic necessity.

She felt herself lifted, his arms carrying her easily as he turned toward the stairs. Only then, reluctantly, did his mouth leave hers. Eyes closed, Troy turned her face into his neck, breathing in the scent of his cologne and only vaguely aware that he was carrying her into his bedroom.

Dallas set her gently on her feet beside the turned-down bed, only the lamp on the nightstand proving a soft glow. His hands framing her face tenderly, he feathered kisses across her brow and down her cheek, his thumb gliding back and forth over her lips in a rhythmic little caress.

For a few moments, her eyes still closed, Troy held his wrists as though they were lifelines. Then the fever demanded more, and as her eyes slowly opened, her hands were reaching to push the

jacket off his shoulders. The garment fell un-
heeded to the floor as he shrugged out of it, his
hands returning briefly to her face before helping
her to unbutton his white shirt. The tie was
thrown aside, followed by the shirt, and Troy discovered a new fascination in the muscled strength
of his tanned chest.

She reached out tentatively, her fingers thread-
ing among the springy dark hairs to find the firm
flesh beneath, and then she leaned forward suddenly to press her lips to him. She felt her hair
falling free as his fingers dislodged the pins, and
stepped out of her shoes automatically as he
reached for the knot at her shoulder. Shimmering
gold material slid down her body with a whispering sound to pool around her feet, and she heard
Dallas catch his breath sharply.

"God, you're beautiful," he rasped softly, his
eyes avidly searching out the curves shadowed
and highlighted in the dim light.

Golden eyes gazed up at him dreamily for a
moment, and then Troy slid her arms around his
waist and pressed her body against his with a
need beyond reason. Instinct fueled by desire
made her languid movement far more sensual

than she knew, and the strength in her lithe body added an unusual grace.

Dallas caught his breath harshly again, holding her to him fiercely for a moment before lifting her up into his arms and placing her on the bed.

Troy lay silently and watched with passion-dazed eyes as he hastily removed the remainder of his clothing. She felt neither embarrassed nor uncomfortable beneath the intensity of his stare; instead, something deep inside of her burst from seed and bloomed in a new awareness of her own womanhood. Something was unleashed, and the sound released from her throat as he moved down on the bed beside her was a sound born in the caves.

She felt the sensual abrasiveness of his hands as they shaped and molded willing flesh, and when he buried his face between her breasts, Troy tangled her fingers in his hair and gave herself up to pleasure. She didn't realize that she had murmured something aloud until Dallas lifted his head and looked down at her with a curiously arrested expression in his hot eyes.

"What?" he murmured, one hand reaching to trace the clean line of her jaw.

Troy smiled at him a little uncertainly. "I said . . . no lovers. There are no lovers in my past, Dallas."

He went so still that Troy was frightened for an eternal moment, but then he was kissing her with a new intensity and her fear disappeared.

"I was so afraid," he muttered, "of ghosts. They tortured me, because I knew you had to care for them. They haunted me. . . ."

Troy kept her fingers locked in his hair when his lips returned to her breasts, her body arching with a mind of its own at the first touch. Her eyes closed, and she shut out everything but the feel of his lips caressing, his tongue swirling hungrily. A moan rose up from the deepest part of her and escaped in a choked sound as his fingers probed erotically, and a restlessness prodded her toward something she'd never known before.

Her hands moved to grip his shoulders fiercely as his lips trailed slowly down her flat stomach; she lost her breath and couldn't seem to find it again, but it didn't matter. Nothing mattered except his erotic caresses and the splintering tension that was building inside of her until she wanted to scream aloud with the awful pleasure of it. She wanted to move, had to move, but her feverish body wouldn't obey her, and Dallas was creating sensations she wouldn't have believed possible.

She heard her voice pleading with him wildly, passionately, and she suddenly had to hold on to him with all the strength in her supple body because she was afraid she'd be lost if she didn't; lost and soaring with nothing binding her to earth. . . .

And then suddenly he was with her completely, and her eyes widened in the primitive shock of being known so totally. But there was no time to wonder at the feeling or explore it, there was only the building tension stretching like a live wire until something had to give.

Troy cried out when the wire snapped, astonished and overwhelmed by the feelings ripping through her, dimly hearing Dallas groan out her name. . . .

She was not going to open her eyes. She was comfortable, her head pillowed on his shoulder and one hand resting on his chest, and she didn't care if she never moved again. He'd pulled the covers up around them, and the room was no longer filled with the sounds of their harsh breathing; there was only a dreamy aftermath, and Troy savored it.

"Did I call you a lady?" Dallas murmured in a bemused voice. "Maybe I should amend that to read wildcat."

"Complaining?" Troy questioned idly.

"*Hell*, no," he said firmly, and she giggled.

"It was quite a shock to me too."

His hand felt around beneath the covers for a moment, settling on her hip, which he patted gently. "And thereby hangs a tale," he said with relish.

Troy choked back a laugh. "It isn't my fault that you jumped to conclusions," she reminded him. "I said that I *could* have had scores of lovers, not that I did."

"Love makes a man paranoid," he explained apologetically.

"Mmm. Well, let me tell you that I wasn't very flattered by the assumption."

"I'm sorry."

"You sound it."

"Shall I abase myself?"

"Hold on to that thought."

"It's slippery."

"Look, I let you beat me at chess, so—"

"You *let* me?"

"I knew that'd wake you up."

"Witch."

"That's right. I'm a card-carrying, broom-riding, spell-casting, caldron-stirring witch. Better watch your step."

Dallas laughed on a sigh. "Sweetheart, I fell under your spell the night I found a cat burglar in the library."

"And just look what happened to me," she mourned.

"You were ravished."

"I'll say."

He swatted her gently.

"And I was beaten too."

"Not yet."

"Oh, is that going to be a surprise for later?"

"I'm considering it."

"How creative."

"I'm also considering chaining you to this bed until you agree to marry me," Dallas said thoughtfully. "But since you're so good with burglar's tools...."

"I'm glad you remembered that. You've already got a charge of abduction hanging over your head; no need to add incarceration with intent to ravish."

"I abducted you with permission."

"I think that's a contradiction in terms."

"The point stands."

"We'll quibble about it later."

"What shall we quibble about now?"

"Breakfast."

"It's the middle of the night," Dallas protested.

"I know, but you said tomorrow was Mrs. Bradley's day off."

"So?"

"So who's going to fix breakfast?"

"You mean, you aren't?" he asked, horrified.

"I think we've got a problem here."

"You can't cook?"

"There's been so much else to learn," Troy explained solemnly.

"I see."

"Can you cook?" she asked.

"In a pinch."

"You're elected."

"Gee, thanks."

"You're welcome. And while we're at it—"

"While we're at it," he interrupted severely, "you managed to rather neatly evade my proposal. And I even swept you off your feet and ordered moonlight this time."

"Was that a proposal?" Troy asked interestedly. "It sounded more like you had lecherous designs on my body."

"That too."

"A package deal, huh?"

"Right. You'll get a husband who adores you and can't let you walk past without grabbing your—"

"And what'll you get?" she interrupted hastily, swallowing a laugh.

"You." The teasing fell away; he was suddenly grave and tender. "For better or worse . . . for the rest of our lives. You'll be a thorn in my flesh, and a look in my eyes no one else will understand. You'll drive me crazy with your independence, and captivate me again and again with the warmth of you. I'll fight a constant battle to remember that I can't lock you away and keep you all to myself, and I'll love you all the more for that. I'll have to put up with your insane driving, your hot temper, and your nocturnal activities because all of that is a part of you, and part of the reason I love you."

Troy had lifted her head and opened her eyes at last, staring deeply into his blue eyes and wondering dimly if her guardian angel had sent a stranger searching for something to read in the dead of night.

With difficulty she swallowed the lump in her throat. "It sounds," she murmured, "as if you're asking for nothing but trouble."

Dallas smiled and brushed a strand of hair from her face, his other arm tightening around her. "No. I don't expect it to be easy, but I wouldn't have it any other way." He laughed softly, a mere thread of sound. "Oh, sweetheart, I really think you have no idea of just how much I love you. I'm not a violent man, but I'd kill for you. Not a jealous man, but I have to fight the urge to keep you beside me every moment. What I thought was obsession in the beginning was love, and it's gotten stronger with every day that's passed." He hesitated, then added, "I can't...imagine the rest of my life without you beside me."

"Dallas..."

"I know you still need time, Troy. And I want you to be sure. I never thought half a loaf was better than no bread; I have to know that I have all of your love or I'll get out of your life. Of course, I'll be hard to convince when it comes to getting out of your life—"

"*Will* you let me get a word in?"

He looked at her a bit warily. "There goes that temper."

She glared at him. "I was about to say something before you decided to be so damn understanding about giving me more time."

Dallas raised an eyebrow at her. "If you don't like the understanding, I'll try the caveman routine. I never thought there was a caveman inside of me, but since I met you—"

"Dallas."

"I'm all ears."

Suddenly, ruefully, Troy laughed. "Damn. I really broke the mood, didn't I?"

"With a vengeance. It's a good thing I don't have a fragile ego," he told her philosophically.

Troy sighed, beginning to doodle among the hairs on his chest. It was fascinating to watch. "I just wanted to—to point out that I never would have accepted the ring if I hadn't been sure." She looked up, her eyes shining gold. "Dallas, I love you with everything inside of me. I can't imagine a life without you either."

"Troy..."

She laughed a little unsteadily. "Now don't start arranging the wedding, all right? We have time."

Dallas gently pulled her head down to rest on his chest, holding her close. "So you want to spend the rest of your life with me," he said chidingly, "but you aren't sure we're ready for marriage, is that it?"

"Well..."

"Is this the woman I called a lady?"

"I thought you'd already amended that."

"Maybe I should." He chuckled softly, the sound a rumble in her ear. "Never mind, sweetheart; I'll get you to the altar eventually."

"Such confidence."

"Always."

"Dallas?"

"Hmm?"

"I really do love you."

He hugged her tightly. "I love you, too, Troy."

She drifted off to sleep, her restless nature oddly at peace.

"Are you going to sleep all day?"

Dallas forced his eyes open, battling his normal early-morning reluctance to greet the day. For a moment his mind was totally blank, but then he remembered the night and day before and a sudden energy and awareness raced through him. He pushed himself up on an elbow, realizing only then that Troy had been awake for quite a while.

She was kneeling beside him on the bed, bright-eyed, her glorious hair tumbled, looking amazingly sexy dressed in his white shirt and nothing else. Dallas reached for her.

Troy stopped him with a hand placed on his chest. "Breakfast."

"That's what I was reaching for," he said, wounded.

She frowned at him reprovingly, then twisted around to reach for a large lap tray at the foot of the bed. "C'mon, sit up, get comfortable. This may very well be a one-shot deal; better take advantage of it."

Surprised, Dallas stared down at the very inviting breakfast laid out on the tray. A fluffy omelet, bacon, toast, juice, coffee—all perfectly prepared. "You lied to me!" he accused. "You said you couldn't cook."

Troy picked up a piece of bacon and smiled sunnily at him. "I never lie. I was just pulling your leg."

"Well—"

She held up a hand quickly. "Please. No off-color remarks so early in the morning."

"You started it."

"Eat your breakfast."

"I see you're going to be a bossy wife."

Troy didn't rise to the bait. "Eat your breakfast," she repeated calmly.

Dallas quickly discovered that she'd been pulling his leg with a vengeance, because she was a very good cook. He ended up sharing the food with her, even though she protested that she never ate very much in the morning. Then they shared a bath in the huge tub that had tempted Troy once before.

"I keep expecting a sign to flash FASTEN SEAT BELTS," she said in a bemused voice.

"What?"

"Well, there are enough gadgets in this tub to fly a jet plane. This, for instance. What's it for?"

"Bubbles."

"Really? Let's have some."

Dallas started laughing. "That huge house of yours, and not a single Jacuzzi?"

"Nope. I've always relied on utilitarian showers."

He watched her in fascination as she luxuriated among the bubbles and made no attempt to hide her utter enjoyment of a new experience. Dallas shook his head. "You are the oddest mixture of sophistication and innocence," he murmured. "Just when I think you can't surprise me, you do. I'll never get bored growing old with you, sweetheart."

Darkly she said, "I'm going to turn into a prune instead of growing old, because I don't want to get out of this tub."

He laughed again. "You can stay here only until I finish shaving; then I pull the plug."

"I'll fight you for it," she declared.

A gleam was born in his eyes. "On second thought maybe I'll wait to shave."

"Dallas? Good heavens, that's ... that's kinky."

"Complaining?" he murmured.

"Hell, no ... "

"Were you serious about being my backup man on the next job?" she asked quite some time later as she hung up the phone after a brief conversation with Jamie.

Dallas, sprawled out on the couch in the den, looked at her warily. "For my sins, yes."

She lifted an eyebrow at him. "Busy tonight?"

"I think I'll be busy learning how to burgle tonight. Dressed all in black, I assume?"

"Uh-huh."

He looked reflective. "I've always wondered about that. The dressing in black, I mean. Is it just to blend in with the darkness?"

Cheerfully she said, "It's mostly that. Also, it

tends to scare the hell out of someone to turn on a light and see a stranger dressed in black."

Dallas frowned at her for a moment, then nodded. "I see. They're bound to hesitate, and that gives you an edge."

She nodded. "And time. More than once, those few seconds of astonishment have given me time to get out the window."

"Shouldn't the police be looking for a lady cat burglar by now? Since you've been seen, I mean?"

"You forget; the people I burgle don't dare call the police. It would be a trifle awkward for them to explain that their stolen property was stolen from them."

He grinned a little. "You have the best of things, don't you? The police probably know what you're doing, and they look the other way: and your victims don't dare press charges for fear of going to jail themselves."

Troy looked at him gravely. "You're still not quite comfortable with what I do, are you?"

"No," he said honestly, catching her hand and pulling her down to his side. "But I'm coming to terms with it. I know that your fee goes to charity, and God knows you aren't in it for financial gain anyway—"

"How did you know—" Troy broke off and answered her own question ruefully. "Your little setup. Chris Jordan told you that I wanted the fee given to charity."

"He was a bit bewildered by that," Dallas said wryly.

"Most of my clients are," Troy explained, "because most of them live outside this area and don't know me socially."

Dallas looked at her curiously. "Where's the most distant place you've traveled to—uh—burgle?"

"Actually to break into a house," she told him tranquilly, "it was South America. But I've done some—work in Europe and the Orient."

"What kind of *work*?" Dallas asked in the tone of a man who wasn't quite sure he wanted to know.

Troy patted him reassuringly on the cheek. "Don't worry, darling; I was helping the police—" Before she could finish the sentence, Dallas had caught her in a fierce hug.

"That's the first time you've called me that," he

said huskily. "And right now, I don't care if you were helping the Mafia."

Returning the hug with interest, she murmured absently, "The Mafia isn't terribly interested in art objects; they're far more intrigued by the higher-profit crimes."

Dallas smiled wryly at her as he sat back on the couch. "You know a lot about crime and criminals, don't you, sweetheart?"

"The mark of a professional," she told him solemnly, "is research."

"And yet you're not cynical. That's . . . odd."

Troy looked thoughtful. "Well, crime and sin have always been with us and probably always will be; the only problem I see in dealing with them is confusing the two. What I do may be a crime technically, but it isn't a sin. I don't feel guilty about it, and I'm not ashamed of it."

"You're amazing."

She gave him a startled look.

"Really," he insisted. "Because you know yourself the way very few people ever manage to. And because your eyes are wide open and yet you don't hesitate to do what you can to help rather than bemoan the fact that the world's going to hell in a handbasket." He smiled crookedly. "I saw a poster once that ran something like: *Somebody do something! Oh . . . I'm somebody*. There's no startled realization for you, Troy; you know you're somebody, and you do something about any problem you see."

Troy gazed at him for a moment, then slid her arms around him and hugged. Hard. "Thank you," she murmured.

"Don't mention it," he said huskily.

A few moments later she asked idly, "Are you sure you want to be a burglar tonight?"

"I'd consider it an honor," he said determinedly, and Troy giggled.

"You sound like you're going before a firing squad."

"Visions of irate, burgled victims are dancing in my head."

"The victim won't be at home. That's why Jamie called me; we've had our eye on this place for weeks, but the security system's been a hard nut to crack."

"And now?"

"We have it on the best authority that the owner's leaving the city briefly with half his security force, and leaving the painting we want behind."

"Whose authority?"

"His butler's."

Dallas choked on a laugh. "You have no scruples! What'd you do, bribe the guy?"

Troy swallowed another giggle and replied sedately, "No; Bryce got him drunk." When Dallas choked again, she said gravely, "There's an entire underground network of information channels through the domestic staffs in this city. It's incredible, really. And Bryce has gotten the fine art of subtly extracting information down pat by now. He's terrific."

Looking toward the heavens in a plea, Dallas murmured, "She's even corrupted her butler. The British lion is having its tail yanked by an upstart American lady cat burglar."

"I resent that."

"Which?"

"Upstart. The British stopped calling us Colonials that years ago."

"Don't you believe it."

She giggled. "Besides, my French ancestry is

awfully close to the surface, you know. And
Daddy was half Irish."

Dallas groaned. "You had to throw that into
the pot. No wonder you have such a temper; if
there's a more combustible mixture than Irish and
French, I don't know what it is."

"I do."

"You do what?"

"Know a more combustible mixture."

"Yeah? What?"

"A scrupulously legal but ruthless businessman
and a lady cat burglar."

"There is that."

"Yes."

"Wanna go up in flames?"

"I thought you'd never ask...."

For Dallas's first active experience with her
work, Troy had deliberately chosen a job promising to be one of the more difficult waiting in the
wings. The inborn caution that had made her hesitate all this time wanted, not for Dallas to prove
anything, but for him to understand completely
and believe in what she did. She knew very well

that a part of his reserve was due to the dangers involved; she also knew that if she'd been a cop or firefighter, that reserve would have been the same.

It was perhaps, she thought in amusement, a bit much to expect a man to accept amicably that his wife was a cat burglar—even a semilegitimate one. But she felt she had to try.

However, she really hadn't planned on their first midnight expedition together turning into a comedy of errors....

"*Damn.*" Troy wailed softly.

"What?" Dallas hissed as he crouched beside her outside a formidable wrought-iron fence. It was just past the witching hour of midnight.

"You're not going to believe this. *I* don't believe this," she muttered. "I forgot my flashlight."

Dallas tried to resist the temptation and failed. "You're supposed to be the expert at this," he pointed out maddeningly in a whisper.

She glared at him in the now-and-again cloud-shrouded moonlight. "I *am*. It's all your fault; if you hadn't distracted me by nibbling on my neck while I was getting the tools together—"

"With the prospect of five to ten staring me in the face, I didn't know when I'd get another chance to nibble," he defended himself calmly.

Troy ignored that. "I don't suppose you brought a flashlight?"

"Sorry."

"Fine pair of thieves we are," she grumbled, glancing at her watch and waiting for Jamie to signal that the electrified fence had been switched off.

"Don't remind me."

"Business mogul caught hobnobbing with lady cat burglar: film at eleven."

"Cute."

"Don't worry; it'll be a first offense."

"Oh, great."

Troy fought back a giggle, reminding herself sternly that they were here to do a job. The Handie-Talkie clipped to her belt buzzed softly, and she thumbed on the mike.

"It's off," Jamie announced, still sounding amused—as he had ever since they'd gone over the plans at Dallas's house. "*Bon voyage*, you two."

Dallas grimaced as she responded with a soft "Okay" and replaced the device on her belt.

"Does he have to sound so damn cheerful?" he muttered.

"He thinks it's funny that scrupulously legal Dallas Cameron is about to break into a house," Troy murmured.

Remaining heroically silent, Dallas gave her a boost over the fence, holding his breath until she had successfully negotiated the spikes and now-dead electrified wire at the top.

Troy, safely on the inside, watched him as he leaped easily and caught the base of two spikes, pulling himself up and over with an admirable economy of movement. As he landed with a soft thud beside her, she said approvingly, "You did that very well. A born thief."

He swatted her on the fanny. "Any more editorial comments and I'm going to get violent," he warned.

She sighed. "I knew I shouldn't have invited you along: you're spoiling the party."

"Shall we get this over with, please?"

The first electronic camera was encountered about a hundred yards into the enclosure, sobering them both. It was panning back and forth slowly, like all the cameras around the perimeter of the place, calling for split-second timing in getting past undetected. Careful planning paid off; they got through, Troy thought, with at least an even chance of not having been seen.

Once past two layers—fence and cameras—of outer security, they encountered the final layer outside the house. And it was one that Dallas had not been looking forward to.

The dogs.

Never one to wait for trouble to find her, Troy halted at the edge of the trees bordering the yard and pulled a high-frequency whistle from her belt. "I hope we have the right frequency," she muttered.

"You mean you're not sure?" Dallas asked in alarm.

"Everything in life's a gamble."

"I don't find that very comforting."

Troy blew through the whistle, adding calmly, "Not being reckless to the point of insanity, however, I took the precaution of making friends with these two a couple of weeks ago. Let's hope they remember me."

The dogs came bounding up seconds later. They were large, lean, and appeared as hostile as

Dobermans were reputed to be. They were wearing spiked collars, and announced their presence with rumbling growls.

"Hi, guys," Troy said cheerfully, stepping forward into the yard.

Dallas stepped forward also, irresistibly reminded of the night they'd met and the bored Doberman that had given him a bad moment while Troy had clung to the wall. These two animals were the opposite of bored: they were both alert and sniffed suspiciously at the two intruders strolling casually toward the house.

"Heel," Troy said firmly, making a slight motion with one hand as she continued walking.

The dogs immediately took up position on either side of her, pacing along silently.

Dallas glanced down at the dog between him and Troy. "Not that I'm complaining, mind you, but they accepted us awfully quickly."

"Be thankful they're guard dogs and not attack dogs," she murmured. "The latter don't obey anyone but their handlers."

Suddenly conscious of the silent yard and darkened house, Dallas lowered his voice. "I'm glad—

believe me. Now, are you sure that the security guards aren't on tonight?"

"Reasonably."

"Troy—"

"I'm sure, I'm sure. The security guards went with the owner, his wife, and her diamonds. They'll only be gone one night, and he's depending on the dogs, the house's electronic security system, and the perimeter cameras—which are tied in to TV sets in the gatehouse down there by the road. The single guard monitoring the sets is a mystery buff, and he picked up a nice, thick, bloodcurdling paperback this afternoon on his way to work." She sent Dallas an amused look. "Satisfied?"

"With your preparation—certainly," he responded promptly. "It's all the unknown factors—like sheer bad luck—that worry me."

"Stop worrying. From here on it's a piece of cake. That window up there on the second floor has a defective catch; it's been temporarily disconnected from the security system. The safe is in the room across the hall: it's wired, but the alarm can be bypassed without disturbing the rest of the system. And a five-year-old could get the safe open in nothing flat."

Dallas shook his head slightly. "Where *do* you get all this information?"

"Trade secret," she murmured, halting a few feet from the house to look upward to the second floor. Absently she held out a hand to him. "Let me have the rope."

There was a moment of silence.

"I thought you had it," Dallas said finally in a muffled voice.

She turned slowly to stare at him, fighting an insane urge to sink down on the ground and laugh herself silly. Then she sighed. Keeping her voice even with an effort, she said, "We'd better start searching."

"For what?" he asked unsteadily.

"A ladder, dammit."

NINE

FROM THAT MOMENT on the evening went rapidly downhill in a comical slide crossed abruptly with the shock of dangerous reality. Troy had no intention of crossing the no-man's-land of cameras and fence more than once again, so she discounted her mind's logical suggestion to go back to the fence and summon Jamie to bring a rope.

They looked for a ladder and found one in a simply locked outbuilding. Muttering to herself, Troy picked the lock with Dallas looking on interestedly.

The ladder made the Dobermans nervous, and

they had to spend a few moments soothing the dogs. Then, having agreed beforehand that Dallas would remain—reluctantly—outside to keep the dogs calm, Troy went easily up the ladder to the second-floor window with the defective catch.

And found that the catch was defective, all right; it resisted her best efforts to unlock it.

After a frustrating ten minutes Troy leaned an elbow on the top rung and looked down. Dallas, who was holding the base of the ladder steady, and both dogs stared up at her. Torn between laughter and the wry realization that *of course*, nothing would go right just when she wanted him to see how smoothly everything *could* go, Troy ignored an impulse just to leave.

"The Fates are against me," she hissed down to him.

"What's the problem?" he whispered back.

"Name it. Just name it."

"I could find a rock."

Troy bent back to her task with determination. "I'm going to get this thing open," she muttered, "even if we have to stay here all night."

Twenty minutes later the catch finally gave with a rusty click, and Troy very carefully pried the window open. With a quick, reassuring wave to Dallas, she disappeared into the house.

Dallas leaned against the ladder and gazed down at his restless canine companions, then looked up at the suddenly clear, moonlit sky with a grimace. Great. Just great. All they needed was for the lone guard to decide to take a stroll and spot the ladder propped up against the side of the house.

Troy came back to the window. She made absolutely no sound, and only the dogs' sudden attention sparked his own as Dallas looked toward the window. Elbow resting on the sill, Troy looked down at him with an indefinable expression on her face. "This has ceased to be funny," she called down to him in a voice nonetheless filled with laughter.

"What now?"

"The safe isn't where it's supposed to be."

After a moment Dallas said ruefully, "Sweetheart, can we please discuss some other occupation for you?"

Troy sighed. "I just wanted to warn you that this is going to take a while. I may have to comb the whole damn house."

"This ladder is standing out like a peacock in a chicken coop," he observed. "There's not a cloud in the sky now."

"Take it down and lay it up against the house," she suggested. "I'll sing out when I need it again."

"Sure?"

"I'm sure." She disappeared from the window a second time.

Dallas carefully let the ladder down and placed it against the brick wall, softly reassuring the two increasingly nervous dogs. He was fighting hard not to laugh; not even the seriousness of the situation could detract from his enjoyment of Troy's comic despair.

She wasn't gone long enough for Dallas to begin to worry. Nearly half an hour later, he heard her voice breathlessly commanding, "Catch!" and a neatly rolled painting dropped into his hands. Then, before he could do more than make a slight movement toward the ladder, he saw that she was coming out the window ladder or no ladder.

"Hey!"

"Now get ready to catch me!" she directed, still breathless as she clung to the outside wall and hung on to the windowsill, hastily pulling the sash down as far as possible without lowering it on her gripping hand.

"The ladder—"

"No time!" She lowered herself cautiously until her booted feet were nearly within his reach, then whispered, "Here I come," and let go.

Dallas caught her with no problem, although the force of her fall caused him to stagger back and sideways in a crazy little step to avoid the inquisitive dogs. He immediately set her on her feet, accepting the need for haste without question.

Softly Troy commanded the dogs to stay, then led the way quickly and quietly across the yard and into the woods. "They'll get restless in a minute," she murmured, still moving swiftly. "We'd better be past the cameras, over the wall, and gone when they do."

Both remained silent while they traversed the woods and eased through the camera-watched corridor. In fact, neither said another word until they were both over the fence and nearly a block away, where Jamie was waiting patiently in his car.

Troy spoke a few brief words to Jamie after

handing over the painting so that he could return it to its proper owner the next day. Dallas saw the older man shoot a quick, searching look at her face, and he, too, was concerned by the oddly distant sound of her voice. But Jamie said nothing about his obvious worry, and neither did Dallas until they had gone on to his car and were heading for home.

"What happened back there?" he asked finally, quietly, very conscious of the distance she'd abruptly put between them.

She was silent for a moment, then stirred slightly. "The house wasn't empty," she said slowly; only her profile was visible to him in the darkness of the car.

"What happened?" he repeated tensely.

"I spent fifteen minutes dodging a guard," she murmured in that oddly thoughtful, distant voice. "An armed guard."

Dallas felt a sudden chill as he thought of what could have happened to her. His hands tightened on the wheel, and visions of guards with nervous trigger fingers and guns fired hastily in darkness flashed before him.

"He didn't see me," she went on almost absently. "But he was heading upstairs toward that bedroom when I came out the window." She toyed absently with the ski mask still tucked in her belt because she hadn't thought they would need to cover their faces.

"Troy—" Dallas broke off abruptly, fighting the hardest battle he'd ever fought with himself in an effort to overcome instincts and fears. The natural instinct to wrap a loved one in cotton wool was one he could deal with intellectually; the very real fear for that loved one's life was something entirely different. He had promised that he'd never ask her to be less than she was, and he meant to keep that promise.

But conflicting emotions and thoughts raced through him. He was proud of Troy, of her abilities and her cool courage. If they'd lived in the days when danger was a constant companion, he would have gloried in the sure knowledge of her fighting by his side. But they didn't live in those days. Neither of them had to fight for survival, and both had already fought to achieve a certain success in their lives and their businesses.

The difference was that Troy was still fighting, and hers was a potentially dangerous fight. She didn't fight to prove that she could, or to assert her competence as a woman. No, she had simply looked around years ago and seen an imbalance, an injustice that her particular talents and abilities were suited to combat. So she fought.

There was nothing wrong with that.

But it wasn't *right* either, Dallas thought dimly, trying to untangle the chaotic threads of reason and emotion. Did he believe it wasn't right because women weren't meant to face the lions of life? They were the builders and givers of life, he reasoned, and it was ironic that life so often saw fit to challenge their basically gentle natures. But if challenged, they fought, and with a strength and courage usually hidden beneath soft exteriors.

The image returned of a woman with a baby on one hip and a rifle on the other, fighting for what was hers, soft eyes turned steely, graceful body taut. Women were born with the innate ferocity of the she-cat protecting her young, and they understood that even if their men did not.

Given a choice, though, Dallas felt, most would hand the guns over to their men and cuddle their babies close. Not because they were weaker than men, or less brave, but just because they were different. Nature had designed men and women to complement one another, not to be the same.

Dallas gradually focused his thoughts on the specific: Troy. She fought her battle with a dedication that could never be belittled. And she balanced the baby and the gun, giving so much of her time to charities, then donning the tools of a dangerous trade and helping people in another way.

But how much, he wondered, could one woman be asked to give? Granted, she'd made the choice herself, and he had to respect that. She had spent five years balanced tautly on the brink of discovery . . . exposure . . . danger.

And she wanted to go on.

"Dallas?"

Yanked back to the present, he realized in surprise that the car was parked in his drive. Without a word he got out of the car and came around to her door, opening it for her.

Troy, her face still and a little watchful, accepted his help and then accompanied him up the walk, as silent as he. Once in the house, Dallas went immediately into the den and crossed to a built-in bar in one corner. He looked inquiringly at Troy, accepted her slight shake of the head as an answer, then splashed whiskey into a glass.

She slowly unfastened her tool belt and dropped it onto an end table, moving around to sit on the couch. Watching him and thinking that the black turtleneck sweater and slacks gave him a rakish, compellingly sexy air over and above his good looks, she heard her voice emerge in a neutral tone.

"You're not going to ask me to give it up, are you?"

He shook his head silently, staring down at the glass in his hand for a second before draining it quickly.

"Why?" she asked.

"I promised," he answered bleakly.

"And you wish you hadn't." It wasn't a question.

Dallas set the empty glass down with controlled force, then crossed the room to sit down beside her. "And I wish I hadn't," he agreed flatly.

She looked at him gravely. "We can't live with that between us."

"I know."

Troy waited silently because she knew from his

brooding expression that Dallas had come to some conclusion, some decision about them. And she wondered what he would say and wondered if his words could straighten out the confused tangle of her own thoughts.

He reached for her hand, holding it firmly, and when he spoke, it was obvious that he was weighing each word carefully.

"Troy, I know—I believe—that the kind of job you did tonight is a necessary one. There are loopholes in our justice system that tie the hands of the police in some cases, and a lot of innocent people are hurt by them."

He took a deep breath and looked at her levelly. "But I can't live with the knowledge of your being in that kind of danger. I just can't. If tonight had gone—according to plan, maybe I wouldn't have realized it so clearly for a while. Maybe I would have convinced myself that the danger was slight—for a while. But not for long.

"Tonight *didn't* go according to plan though. I saw the danger to you, and I know that I can't live with it." Dallas hesitated, then smiled a small and crooked smile. "But I promised, didn't I? So I'm not going to ask you to quit. And please understand that I'm not trying emotional blackmail by telling you that I can't take it. I'm being as honest as I know how."

He gazed at her intently. "But I want to ask you something else, sweetheart. I want to ask you . . . if there's time in your life for us."

She returned his look, a slow realization growing in her own, and Dallas nodded slightly.

"You see it, too, don't you? Troy, you fill your life to bursting with your work and with helping people. And there's nothing wrong with that. But there's you, too. Me. Us. I think we're pretty important. I think we deserve the time to build our lives together."

"Something has to . . . go," she said slowly.

"Don't think of it that way," he insisted quietly. "Look at all the people you've helped. Remember that some of the world's most beautiful and precious art objects are with their rightful owners because of you. You believed that you could make a difference and you *did*. But that was a part of your life that was never meant to last forever. It's something you should always remember with pride because you cared enough to fight against a problem. Remember it—and go on."

His hand tightened on hers. "Share my life, sweetheart. You won't be less than you are; you could never be that." His free hand lifted to cup her cheek warmly. "I love you, Troy."

Troy stared at him, a deeper understanding in her eyes. But she couldn't put it into words just yet, and she needed somehow to put it into words. Leaning forward, she slipped her arms around his neck and rested her head on his shoulder. "I think," she murmured softly, feeling his arms go around her, "I've made my choice. But I have to work it through. D'you mind?"

After a moment Dallas rose easily, holding her in his arms. "I don't mind. Just . . . stay with me while you're working it through."

She held on to him tightly as he carried her upstairs to their bed.

Days passed, and if Dallas was troubled by Troy's silence on the subject of their future together, he said nothing about it. The demands of their respective companies reared their heads a few days later, giving both of them a thoughtful new perspective on their compatibility.

Having tagged along during some of Troy's very full days, Dallas invited her to accompany him to his office whenever she could; since her hours were flexible, she usually accepted.

At the office Troy observed for the first time the full force of his personality as he directed a large staff and the company's work on government contracts. With her background in electronics, she found his job far from alien, and she got to ask questions about another part of a scientific, technical business that had always fascinated her.

She became a familiar figure around his office, getting to know most of his staff and causing havoc, Dallas swore, to his self-control.

"Should I leave?" she asked politely when he made the accusation.

Dallas, who'd just closed the door to his office, rather pointedly locked it before crossing the room to join her on the comfortable couch along one wall. "Don't you dare," he said firmly.

"It isn't five o'clock yet," she protested weakly a moment later.

"So?"

"I thought we were going to be businesslike during the day."

"Best-laid plans..."

"Dallas? Darling, the gossip columns are having a field day with us now; d'you want your staff to join the throng in speculation?"

"They already have." He was busily exploring her throat.

"They have? Uh...what're they doing?"

"Betting. I'm not supposed to know about it, you understand, but there's a rather large bet on the date of the wedding."

Troy was going to ask him what the odds-on favorite was, but somehow or other she forgot about it....

Not content just to sit in his office, Dallas was usually right in the thick of things. He spent time in the labs, consulting with his engineers and technicians, going over design specifications and the like. And he didn't think twice about rolling up his sleeves and working beside his people.

Troy spent a large amount of her time at his office just watching him. She saw that his staff respected both his business acumen and his knowledge of electronics and that they liked him.

And she saw further evidence of what she already knew—that he was a fair and just man, hearing all sides of a disagreement before making a decision.

During these times, Troy finally worked through her own decision. She'd thought long and hard, not only because the decision had to be made but because she wanted to understand her reasons for making the choice she did. The most important reason, of course, was that she loved Dallas. And she'd finally realized that there was nothing so important in her life that it could overshadow her love for him.

She thought about what he'd said about her nocturnal outings, weighing each word with care. The selfless motives he'd attributed to her work were, she knew, not entirely accurate. Searching herself ruthlessly, she knew that while she had a genuine desire to help people, she'd also derived an enormous satisfaction from pitting her wits and her strength against the odds.

And yet . . . Troy knew that Dallas was right in saying that she'd never meant to go on doing that work forever. Life depended on change: she knew that as well as anyone. And as long as she was being truthful in her inner searching, she admitted to herself that she no longer felt a sense of eagerness when confronted by a job. Perhaps the years brought caution; perhaps the dangers that had sharpened her wits once now gave her pause. She still believed that it was a necessary kind of work, but she began to wonder if there could be an easier way to accomplish it.

In the meantime she stayed with Dallas in his home and reveled in learning the joys of loving and being loved. She discovered how delightful it was to be awakened with kisses, to share a tubful of bubbles, to have a warm and loving man to cuddle up to at night. She grew to understand that she felt more of a woman with Dallas beside her.

There was always a laugh on the tip of her tongue, and never enough time for all the things she wanted to tell him. And the thought of living without him was something she could no longer conceive of.

They spent the weekend together alone, just talking and sharing their ideas. When Dallas tentatively mentioned that he'd often thought of incorporating the development of security systems into his company, Troy decided abruptly that she was being an absolute idiot with all her hesitating.

"I've been thinking," she murmured, lying comfortably beside him on big pillows in front of the fireplace, "about security systems too."

"And?"

"Well, the police are always stressing prevention, right?"

"Right." He was idly playing with her fingers and watching her thoughtful face.

"So I was thinking," she mused, "that maybe I should concentrate on that part of the problem. Prevention, I mean. It wouldn't solve the problem, but it'd go a long way toward helping, don't you think?"

Suddenly very still, Dallas said carefully, "I think it would. But then . . . I'm biased."

"You certainly are." Troy looked at him gravely. "You gave me a lot of very nice motives for having become a cat burglar, and I'd like to think you were at least partly right. But you didn't mention some of the selfish reasons."

He smiled a little. "You mean the excitement, the adventure of it?"

She nodded. "That was a very large part of it, Dallas."

"*Was?*"

"I—don't need that anymore. The five years were thoroughly enjoyable, and I wouldn't change them if I could. But you were right; those years are over. You asked me if—if there'd be time for us, and I know now that nothing is more important than making sure of that."

"Troy..." He held her hand tightly. "Marry me?"

Her free hand lifted to touch his cheek. "Are you kidding?" she said shakily. "I'd be an idiot to pass up the deal you're offering, darling. And even though I've acted like an idiot, I'm not one. I love you, more and more each day. I want to share the rest of my life with you."

Dallas released her hand only to sweep her into his arms, a rumbling groan of relief and happiness escaping. "Thank God. Oh, sweetheart, I was so afraid.... I knew how important your work was to you—"

"Not as important as you," she murmured huskily. "Not as important as us. I love you, Dallas. I think I loved you from that very first meeting. Why else would I have trusted you with the painting?"

He laughed unsteadily. "And you've been a thorn in my flesh since that night; more, you've been a maddening, impossible disease in my blood."

Troy giggled suddenly. "That sounds terrible."

"It was terrible," he whispered, his lips trailing fire down her throat. "And wonderful...and unforgettable...."

"Mmm...darling?"

"Sweetheart?"

"How would you like a business partner?" she mused, barely able to keep her mind on her own words.

Dallas rose to his feet, pulling her up as well. "Why not?" He grinned at her. "You already own stock in the company."

"I didn't tell you that!"

"No, you little witch; you didn't. I had to read it in one of those gossip columns."

"Uh...sorry about that, darling."

"You should be. It was a terrible shock."

"I find that hard to believe."

He frowned down at her severely. "No? How

would it look in a stockholders' report that a former cat burglar owned stock in the company?"

"You'll have a version of the same problem," she pointed out, "if it ever becomes known that your *wife* is a former cat burglar."

Dallas showed her an exaggerated wince. "I'll be a nervous wreck for seven years."

"Seven years?"

"The statute of limitations, remember?"

Troy looked thoughtful. "I'd forgotten that. I suppose I should really do the decent thing and stay out of your life for seven—" She broke off abruptly as she found herself tossed over his shoulder and swatted punishingly on the fanny.

"On the other hand," she murmured in a laugh-filled voice, "who wants to do the decent thing?"

Dallas started purposefully for the stairs. "My sentiments exactly, sweetheart; nobility bores me."

"Which house will we live in?" she asked idly quite some time later as they lay in a lamplit bedroom. "It makes no sense to keep them both."

"I'll leave it up to you," Dallas said over a huge yawn.

"That's not fair; you'll have to live there too!"

"She's being demanding already," he told the celling ruefully.

"Dallas..."

"We'll flip a coin." When she punched him weakly in the ribs, he relented and said more seriously, "I thought you'd probably want to keep your house, since it belonged to your parents."

"Not really. They loved the place, but didn't really spend much time there."

"Mmm. Well, there's no hurry about deciding, is there?"

"No. But I should warn you that Bryce has been with the family all my life."

"I've always wanted a classy English butler. What about Jamie?"

"Jamie," Troy said dryly, "has informed me that he's going to Ireland to spend some time with his family, after which he proposes to take a cruise around the world."

"Tactful, isn't he?"

"Yes. But, Dallas—I'd like to ask him to live with us when he eventually comes back."

"'Sfine with me. Between the two of us, we might even be able to keep you out of trouble."

"I resent that."

"I thought you would."

A sudden thought occurred to Troy. "I wonder how Bryce and Mrs. Bradley will get along?"

"Fine. Unless he tries to get her drunk."

Troy was still giggling when Dallas turned out the lamp on the nightstand and pulled her even closer to his side.

TEN

"I REALIZE," DALLAS said carefully, "that no one at the party could have entertained their suspicions for more than a few fleeting seconds. You understand that I realize that, don't you?"

Troy, sitting cross-legged on their bed, a scantily dressed Buddha in an overlarge football jersey, nodded solemnly as she watched her husband pacing energetically back and forth in front of her. "I understand that you realize that," she confirmed sedately.

Dallas kept pacing. "I mean, just because several of your onetime victims were there is no reason for me to become unduly alarmed, right?"

"Right."

"After all, who in his right mind could believe for one moment that Troy Bennett Cameron could be—or had ever been—a thief? She's a wealthy woman in her own right, married to a wealthy husband, a partner in a very successful company. She's beautiful, very brilliant, and very much a lady. And, to top it all, she's extremely philanthropic. Who'd ever think she could *possibly* have been a thief?"

"Who'd ever think?" Troy parroted faithfully.

"So I realize that if anyone *did* entertain those ridiculous suspicions, it could only have been briefly."

"Uh-huh."

"But I do think, sweetheart," he said, "that for you to appear at a masquerade ball wearing the outfit and tools of a cat burglar was pushing things. Just a bit."

"At the time," Troy murmured apologetically, "it seemed the thing to do."

"And then," Dallas went on conversationally, still pacing, "to lightheartedly demonstrate just how easy it is to pick a lock, open a safe, and by-pass a security system—"

"Tommy's punch. It makes me reckless."

"—seemed to me to be an act far beneath your normal standards of intelligence."

"That'll teach you to work late," she said with obscure satisfaction.

Dallas stopped pacing and, hands on hips, stared down at his erring wife with heroic patience. "It certainly will; I'll never again *meet* you at a party rather than *accompany* you from home. And what, may I ask, happened to Joan of Arc?"

"The armor was awkward," she explained.

"So you decided to go as Troy Bennett, cat burglar par excellence?"

"Madness, I know," she said sadly.

"That's your excuse?"

"Well, there was the thought that it might help drum up business."

"For the police?"

She ignored that splendidly. "And it worked too. Cy Kincaid wants to talk to us Monday about a security system for his home."

"Is this the same Cy Kincaid," Dallas asked

politely, "you relieved of one rather priceless golden figurine a year before you met me?"

"That's him," Troy confirmed sunnily.

Dallas made a muffled sound indicative of despair.

"You did say for better or worse," she reminded gently.

"But not for insanity."

"Sorry."

"And I thought you refused to install security for these art-at-any-price types."

"Kincaid's reformed."

He stared at her suspiciously. "How do you know?"

"A little bird told me."

"Troy..."

"Interpol; they've been watching him ever since. And besides, Dallas, when we install his system, I'll go into my spiel about how no system is foolproof, and about how there's an information network among thieves. And assure him very seriously that the most vulnerable victim of theft in the world is one who can't yell about his loss to the police."

Dallas addressed the ceiling plaintively. "She just keeps stoking the fire beneath us...."

Wifelike, Troy ignored that. "A little extra preventive medicine can't hurt."

"Take your own advice," he suggested ruefully.

"Are you nervous, darling?"

"The possibility of losing my adored wife to our justice system affects me like that," he explained.

"Cat burglars are almost never caught; did you know that? Robbers, yes, but not cat burglars. We're a special breed."

"With special immunity?"

"You're being paranoid, darling. We've been married a year, and nobody's found out yet, have they?"

"Until tonight you maintained a certain— discretion, shall we say?"

"I said I was sorry."

He sat down on the bed and put his head in his hands.

Troy swallowed a giggle. "You have to admit that it's been an exciting year."

"Oh...certainly," he murmured, lifting his head and looking at her with an expression somewhere between mildly bemused and totally petrified. "It certainly has. D'you realize that a year and some-odd weeks ago, I led a perfectly lawful existence?"

"And now you're married to a former cat burglar," she sympathized. "How the mighty are fallen."

"Don't rub it in."

Politely she asked, "D'you want a divorce? You seem to be leading up to that."

"No, I'm merely leading up to a request."

"Really? What is it?"

"Let's avoid masquerades from now on, all right?"

"Of course, darling."

"And ex-victims."

"If you insist."

"And while you're being so generous," he went on in the same calm tone, "could you answer one small question?"

"Which is?"

"Is the fact that my sister had—business—in every city of Tom Elliot's twelve-city concert tour a coincidence?"

"I plead the Fifth Amendment," Troy said immediately.

Dallas lounged back on an elbow and stared at her impenetrable expression. "Sweetheart?"

"Uh-huh?" she said warily.

"Have you been matchmaking behind my back?"

Troy leaned forward suddenly and kissed him, her fingers toying with the towel knotted at his hip. "Have you been seduced lately?" she murmured provocatively.

Temporarily distracted, he mused, "There *was* a crazy lady in my shower this morning."

"Mmm...blow in my ear, and I'll follow you anywhere," she promised huskily, forgetting all about distractions and concentrating only on the marvelous feelings that were always new and exciting.

He didn't exactly blow in her ear, but she followed him anyway to a place outside themselves, a place they both treasured.

A long time later Dallas stirred slightly and tightened his arm around Troy. "You didn't answer my question," he noted with a yawn.

Her voice was muffled against his neck. "What question?"

"Have you been matchmaking behind my back?"

"I never do anything behind your back."

"Troy."

"I introduced them. Sue me. Can I help it if they happen to like each other?"

"It sounds," Dallas said, "more like she's chasing him to me."

"That's a nice brotherly remark."

"I know my sister. When she wants something, she puts on the gloves and steps into the ring."

"*Jumps* into the ring."

"She is chasing him?"

"Well, if you must know, we worked out a campaign."

"Oh, great."

"I warned her that Tommy's a slippery customer, but that just seemed to feed the fire."

"How would you know he's a slippery customer?"

"After ten years of friendship I've seen a lot of girls come and go."

"This is not something a brother needs to hear."

"Don't worry; Andy's got him."

"Is that definite?" Dallas asked politely. "I mean, will she wave a diamond in my face the next time she breezes in?"

"The engagement ring'll be a sapphire," Troy said knowledgeably. "Tommy'll want to match her eyes. But the wedding band will probably be beside it."

"Already?" Dallas said, startled.

"I introduced them three months ago; they're cautious compared to us, darling."

"They'll elope?"

"I wouldn't doubt it. Otherwise Tommy's press agent will probably try to turn it into a circus."

"Has the press agent met Andy?"

"Not yet."

"He doesn't know that he's about to meet his match, then?"

"Nope. It should be fun to watch."

"Only from a concrete bunker."

Troy giggled suddenly. "Speaking of which, did you notice Bryce's shell-shocked expression when we got home?"

"I thought it was my imagination."

"No. While you were taking a shower, I cornered Mrs. Bradley in the kitchen and asked what was going on."

"And?"

"She's trapped him."

"*What?*"

"Her words—not mine."

"You mean . . . ?"

"Uh-huh. They—or rather *she*—is planning a civil ceremony, and we're invited."

Bemused, Dallas said, "You told me Bryce had never married."

"True."

"And Mrs. Bradley's divorced two husbands?"

"Yes."

"Who got who drunk?" Dallas wanted to know.

"I think it was a joint effort."

"Bryce may sneak in tonight and murder us."

"No." Troy choked on a laugh. "He won't have the energy."

Dallas sighed. "What *is* this—an epidemic of matrimony?"

"Nice, isn't it?"

"Mmm. Sweetheart?"

"Yes, darling?"

"Have I told you today how much I love you?"

"No; we were rushed this morning, and you were too mad at me at the party," she said judiciously.

"My excuses?" he asked in amusement.

"Well, I told you today. During lunch in your office. But then you got distracted. . . ."

"That couch comes in handy sometimes," he murmured.

"So you haven't told me today," she reminded reprovingly.

He pulled her easily over on top of him, smiling up at her in the lamplight. "I love you, lady cat burglar. And one day I'll tell our grandchildren that the only thing you ever stole for yourself was my heart."

"And I'll tell them," she whispered adoringly, "that scrupulously legal Dallas Cameron is the only thief who ever beat me at my own game. . . ."

ABOUT THE AUTHOR

KAY HOOPER is the award-winning author of *Blood Dreams, Sleeping with Fear, Hunting Fear, Chill of Fear, Touching Evil, Whisper of Evil, Sense of Evil, Once a Thief, Always a Thief*, the Shadows trilogy, and other novels. She lives in North Carolina, where she is at work on her next book.

Read on for a special preview of
the next thrilling Bishop/Special
Crimes Unit novel, the first in
Kay Hooper's new
Blood trilogy

BLOOD
DREAMS

KAY HOOPER

Available now from Bantam Books

KAY HOOPER

A BISHOP/SPECIAL CRIMES UNIT NOVEL

BLOOD DREAMS

BLOOD DREAMS

On sale now

PROLOGUE

It was the nightmare brought to life, Dani thought.

The vision.

The smell of blood turned her stomach, the thick, acrid smoke burned her eyes, and what had been for so long a wispy dreamlike memory now was jarring, throat-clogging reality. For just an instant she was paralyzed.

It was all coming true.

Despite everything she had done, everything she had *tried* to do, despite all the warnings, once again it was all—

"Dani?" Hollis seemingly appeared out of the smoke at her side, gun drawn, blue eyes sharp even squinted against the stench. "Where is it?"

"I—I can't. I mean, I don't think I can—"

"Dani, you're all we've got. You're all *they've* got. Do you understand that?"

Reaching desperately for strength she wasn't at all sure she had, Dani said, "If somebody had just listened to me when it mattered—"

"Stop looking back. There's no sense in it. Now is all that counts. Which way, Dani?"

Impossible as it was, Dani had to force herself to concentrate on the stench of blood she knew neither of the others could smell. A blood trail that was all they had to guide them. She nearly gagged, then pointed. "That way. Toward the back. But . . ."

"But what?"

"Down. Lower. There's a basement level." Stairs. She remembered stairs. Going down them. Down into hell.

"It isn't on the blueprints."

"I know."

"Bad place to get trapped in a burning building," Hollis noted. "The roof could fall in on us. Easily."

Bishop appeared out of the smoke as suddenly as she had, weapon in hand, his face stone, eyes haunted. "We have to hurry."

"Yeah," Hollis replied, "we get that. Burning building. Maniacal killer. Good seriously outnumbered by evil. Bad situation." Her words and tone were flippant, but her gaze on his face was anything but, intent and measuring.

"You forgot potential victim in maniacal killer's hands," her boss said, not even trying to match her tone.

"Never. Dani, did you see the basement, or are you feeling it?"

"Stairs. I saw them." The weight on her shoulders felt like the world, so maybe that was what was pressing her down. Or ... "And what I feel now ... he's lower. He's underneath us."

"Then we look for stairs."

Dani coughed. She was trying to think, trying to remember. But dreams recalled were such dim, insubstantial things, even vision-dreams sometimes, and there was no way for her to be sure she was remembering clearly. She was overwhelmingly conscious of precious time passing, and looked at her wrist, at the bulky digital watch that told her it was 2:47 P.M. on Tuesday, October 28.

Odd. She never wore a watch. Why was she wearing one now? And why a watch that looked so ... alien on her thin wrist?

"Dani?"

She shook off the momentary confusion. "The stairs. Not where you'd expect them to be," she managed finally, coughing again. "They're in a closet or something like that. A small office. Room. Not a hallway. Hallways—"

"What?"

The instant of certainty was fleeting, but absolute. "Shit. The basement is divided. By a solid wall. Two big rooms. And accessed from this main level by two different stairways, one at each side of the building, in the back."

"What kind of crazy-ass design is that?" Hollis demanded.

"If we get out of this alive, you can ask the architect." The smell of blood was almost overpowering, and Dani's head was beginning to hurt. Badly. She had never before pushed herself for so long without a break, especially with this level of intensity.

It was Bishop who said, "You don't know which side they're in."

"No. I'm sorry." She felt as if she'd been apologizing to this man since she'd met him. Hell, she had been.

Hollis was scowling. To Bishop, she said, "Great. That's just great. You're psychically blind, the storm has all my senses scrambled, and we're in a huge burning building without a freakin' map."

"Which is why Dani is here." Those pale sentry eyes were fixed on her face.

Dani felt wholly inadequate. "I—I don't— All I know is that he's down there somewhere."

"And Miranda?"

The name caused her a queer little shock,

and for no more than a heartbeat, Dani had the dizzy sense of something out of place, out of sync somehow. But she had an answer for him. Of sorts. "She isn't—dead. Yet. She's bait, you know that. She was always bait, to lure you."

"And you," Bishop said.

Dani didn't want to think about that. Couldn't, for some reason she was unable to explain, think about that. "We have to go, now. He won't wait, not this time." *And he's not the only one.*

The conversation had taken only brief minutes, but even so the smoke was thicker, the crackling roar of the fire louder, and the heat growing ever more intense.

Bitterly, Hollis said, "We're on *his* timetable, just like before, like always, carried along without the chance to stop and think."

Bishop turned and started toward the rear of the building and the south corner. "I'll go down on this side. You two head for the east corner."

Dani wondered if instinct was guiding him as well, but all she said to Hollis, was, "He wouldn't take the chance if he had it, would he? To stop and think, I mean."

"If it meant a minute lost in getting to Miranda? No way in hell. That alone would be enough, but on top of that he blames himself for this mess."

"He couldn't have known—"

"Yes. He could have. Maybe he even did. That's why he believes it's his fault. Come on, let's go."

Dani followed, but had to ask. "Do you believe it's his fault?"

Hollis paused for only an instant, looking back over her shoulder, and there was something hard and bright in her eyes. "Yes. I do. He played God one time too many. And we're paying the price for his arrogance."

Again, Dani followed the other woman, her throat tighter despite the fact that, as they reached the rear half of the building, the smoke wasn't nearly as thick. They very quickly discovered, in the back of what might once have been a small office, a door that opened smoothly and silently to reveal a stairwell.

The stairwell was already lighted.

"Bingo," Hollis breathed.

A part of Dani wanted to suggest that they wait, at least long enough for Bishop to check out the other side of the building, but every instinct, as well as the waves of heat at her back, told her there simply wasn't time to wait.

Hollis shifted her weapon to a steady two-handed grip, and sent Dani a quick look. "Ready?"

Dani didn't spare the energy to wonder how anyone on earth could ever be ready for this.

Instead, she concentrated on the only weapon she had, the one inside her aching head, and nodded.

Hollis had only taken one step when a thunderous crash sounded behind them and a new wave of almost intolerable heat threatened to shove them bodily into the stairwell.

The roof was falling in.

They exchanged glances and then, without emotion, Hollis said, "Close the door behind us."

Dani gathered all the courage she could find, and if her response wasn't as emotionless as the other woman's, at least it was steady.

"Right," she said, and closed the door behind them as they began their descent into hell.

One

You had that dream again last night, didn't you?"

Dani kept her gaze fixed on her coffee cup until the silence dragged on a minute longer than it should have, then looked at her sister's face. "Yeah. I had that dream."

Paris sat down on the other side of the table, her own cup cradled in both hands. "Same as before?"

"Pretty much."

"Then *not* the same as before. What was different?"

It was an answer Dani didn't want to offer, but she knew her sister too well to fight the inevitable. "It was placed in time. Two forty-seven in the afternoon, October twenty-eighth."

Paris turned her head to study the wall calendar stuck with South Park character magnets to her refrigerator. "The twenty-eighth, huh? This year?"

"Yeah."

"That's three weeks from today."

"I noticed that."

"Same people?"

Dani nodded. "Same people. Same conversations. Same burning warehouse. Same feeling of doom."

"Except for the time being fixed, it was exactly the same?"

"It's never *exactly* the same. A word changed here or there, a gesture different. I think the gun Hollis carried wasn't the same one as before. And Bishop was wearing a black leather jacket this time."

"But they're always the same. Those two people are always a part of the dream."

"Always."

"People you don't know."

"People I don't know—yet." Dani frowned down at her coffee for a moment, then shook her head and met her sister's steady gaze again. "In the dream, I feel I know them awfully well. I understand them in a way that's difficult to explain."

"Maybe because they're psychic too."

Dani hunched her shoulders. "Maybe."

"And it ended—?"

"Just like it always ends. That doesn't change. I shut the door behind us and we go down the stairs. I know the roof has started collapsing. I know we won't be able to get out the same way we go in. I know something terrible and evil is waiting for us in that basement."

"But you go down there anyway."

"I don't seem to have a choice."

"Or maybe it's a choice you made before you ever set foot in that building," Paris said. "Maybe it's a choice you're making now. The date. How did you see it?"

"Watch."

"On you? You don't wear a watch. You can't."

Still reluctant, Dani said, "And it wasn't the sort of watch I'd wear even if I could wear one."

"What sort of watch was it?"

"It was...military-looking. Big, black, digital. Lots of buttons, more than one display. Looked like it could give me the time in Beijing and the latitude and longitude as well. Hell, maybe it could translate Sanskrit into English, for all I know."

"What do you think that means?"

Dani sighed. "One year of psychology under your belt, so naturally everything has to mean something, I guess."

"When it comes to your dreams, yes, everything means something. We both know that. Come on, Dani. How many times now have you dreamed this same dream?"

"A few."

"A half-dozen times that I know of—and I'm betting you didn't tell me about it right away."

"So?"

"Dani."

"Look, it doesn't matter how many times I've had the dream. It doesn't matter because it isn't a premonition."

"Could have fooled me."

Dani got up and carried her coffee cup to the sink. "Yeah, well, it wasn't your dream."

Paris turned in her chair but remained where she was. "Dani, is that why you came down here, to Venture? Not to keep me company while I go through a messy divorce, but because of that dream?"

"I don't know what you're talking about."

"The hell you don't."

"Paris—"

"I want the truth. Don't make me get it for myself."

Dani turned around, leaning back against the counter as she once again faced the rueful knowledge that she would never be able to keep the truth from her sister, not for long.

Paris wore her burnished copper hair in a shorter style these days—she called it her divorce rebirth—and she was a bit too thin, but otherwise looking at her was like looking into a mirror. Dani had long since grown accustomed to that, and in fact viewed it as an advantage; watching the play of emotions across Paris's expressive face had taught her to hide her own.

At least from everyone except Paris.

"We promised," her sister reminded her. "To leave each other our personal lives, our own thoughts and feelings. And we've gotten very good at keeping that door closed. But I remember how to open it, Dani. We both do."

Dani nodded slowly. "Okay. The dream started a few months ago, back in the summer. When the senator's daughter was murdered by that serial killer in Boston."

"The one they haven't caught yet?"

"Yeah."

Paris was frowning. "I'm missing the connection."

"I didn't think there was one. Which is why I didn't think it was a premonition."

Without pouncing on that admission, her sister said, "Until something changed. What?"

"I saw a news report. The federal agent in charge of the investigation in Boston is the man in my dream. Bishop."

"I still don't see—"

"His wife is Miranda Bishop. Remember her?"

Paris sat up straighter. "It was— What? Nearly a year and a half ago? She's the one who told us about Haven."

"Yeah. She met with us in Atlanta. You and Danny were one argument away from splitting up, and I was between jobs and at loose ends. Neither one of us was interested in becoming a fed, even with the Special Crimes Unit. But working for Haven...that sounded interesting."

Absently, Paris said, "That was the last straw for Danny, you know. When I wanted to use my abilities, when I got a job that actually required them. I saw how creeped-out he was. How could I stay with someone who felt that way about any part of me?"

"Yeah, I know. Been there. Most of the guys I've met couldn't get past the fact that I was an identical twin; having dreams that literally came true hasn't exactly been seen as a fun bonus."

"We are unique."

"Well, sometimes I think being ordinary might have been easier."

"Maybe. Less fun, though." Paris shook her head. "Getting back to your dream—are you saying it has something to do with that serial killer?"

"I think so."

"Why?"

"A feeling."

Paris watched her steadily. "What else?"

Dani didn't want to answer, but finally did. "Whatever was down in that basement was—is—evil. A kind of evil I've never felt before. And one thing that has been the same in every single version of my dream is the fact that it has Miranda."

"She's a hostage?"

"She's bait."

Heartstopping suspense from New York Times *bestselling author*

Kay Hooper

THE WIZARD OF SEATTLE	___28999-2	$7.50/$10.99
AMANDA	___56823-3	$7.50/$10.99
AFTER CAROLINE	___57184-4	$7.50/$10.99
FINDING LAURA	___57185-1	$7.50/$9.99
HAUNTING RACHEL	___57183-7	$7.50/$9.99
STEALING SHADOWS	___57553-8	$7.50/$10.99
HIDING IN THE SHADOWS	___57692-4	$7.50/$10.99
OUT OF THE SHADOWS	___57695-5	$7.50/$10.99
TOUCHING EVIL	___58344-1	$7.50/$10.99
WHISPER OF EVIL	___58346-5	$7.50/$10.99
SENSE OF EVIL	___58347-2	$7.50/$10.99
ONCE A THIEF	___58511-7	$7.50/$10.99
ALWAYS A THIEF	___58568-1	$7.50/$10.99
HUNTING FEAR	___58598-8	$7.50/$10.99
CHILL OF FEAR	___58599-5	$7.50/$9.99
SLEEPING WITH FEAR	___58600-8	$7.50/$9.99
BLOOD DREAMS	___80484-3	$25.00/$32.00
C.J.'S FATE	___59048-7	$6.99/$9.99
THE HAUNTING OF JOSIE	___59047-0	$6.99/$9.99
ILLEGAL POSSESSION	___59053-1	$6.99/$9.99

Please enclose check or money order only, no cash or CODs. Shipping & handling costs: $5.50 U.S. mail, $7.50 UPS. New York and Tennessee residents must remit applicable sales tax. Canadian residents must remit applicable GST and provincial taxes. Please allow 4 - 6 weeks for delivery. All orders are subject to availability. This offer subject to change without notice. Please call 1-800-726-0600 for further information.

Bantam Dell Publishing Group, Inc.	TOTAL AMT	$_____
Attn: Customer Service	SHIPPING & HANDLING	$_____
400 Hahn Road	SALES TAX (NY, TN)	$_____
Westminster, MD 21157		
	TOTAL ENCLOSED	$_____

Name _____

Address _____

City/State/Zip _____

Daytime Phone (_____) _____